Beyond his Time
By Adrian Cousins

Copyright © 2023 Adrian Cousins

All rights reserved. This book or any portion thereof may not be reproduced or used in any manner whatsoever without the author's express written permission except for the use of brief quotations in a book review.

This book is a work of fiction. Names, characters, businesses, schools, places, locales, and incidents are either products of the author's imagination or used in a fictitious manner. Any resemblance to actual persons, living or dead, or actual events is purely coincidental.

www.adriancousins.co.uk

..

Also by Adrian Cousins

The Jason Apsley Series

Jason Apsley's Second Chance

Head of his Time

Force of Time

Calling Time

Beyond his Time

Deana Demon or Diva Series

It's Payback Time

Death Becomes Them

Dead Goode

Standalone Novels

Eye of Time

1

The Shining

After wedging his car in the first available parking bay, Chris hopped out and flung the door closed. Whilst hot-footing across the car park, Chris repeatedly stabbed the lock button on his key fob as he waved it over his shoulder before bounding up the stone steps and into the foyer of the House of Death.

Well, okay, not actually called the House of Death, but rather Waverly House. A care home for the elderly, most of whom would die under its Victorian roof. Although considered by those in the know to be Fairfield's most prestigious residential care home, that didn't negate the residents' inevitable, imminent demise. Bodies strapped to a gurney whilst being trundled out through the front entrance occurred with an almost clockwork regularity – you could set your watch by it. Hence the reason Chris afforded the care home that rather Hitchcock-esque name.

As he barrelled through the entrance, Chris pondered the actual body count. He suspected it would far exceed one of Agatha Christie's many imposing country houses, which

Waverly House would provide a perfect setting for one of her cozy murder mysteries.

The call he'd received earlier from the manager suggested his elderly father would likely be the next body strapped to one of those gurneys. Despite their joint efforts to persuade their father to live with either of them, Chris and his sister had failed. Instead, their eighty-two-year-old father, Jason Apsley, had chosen the House of Death as his preferred option to see out the remainder of his life.

"Hi, Janice," Chris panted. After a short scoot across the car park, his lack of regular exercise resulted in needing to take deep gulps of breath to calm his heart rate. Now in his mid-forties and with a plethora of unused gym membership cards to his name, his athleticism was a far cry from the days of being the school's football and cricket captain. Nevertheless, Megan, his wife of over twenty years, said he was cuddly and there was nothing wrong with love handles.

"Hello, Mr Apsley. I'd heard Miss Shrives had given you a bell. I'm so sorry."

Chris offered a solemn nod in reply to the receptionist before flipping open the cover of the visitors' signing-in book. A weekly event he'd performed for the best part of nearly a year since his father moved here when his dementia reached a level that resulted in being unable to take care of himself. Pouring fabric conditioner into his coffee after washing his bed sheets with a dollop of semi-skimmed had been the final straw. A simple mistake to make, perhaps? However, the said fabric conditioner manufacturer had conjured up the catchy name *Hints of Rainforest*. To those of us fortunate enough to still be in command of all our faculties, the green liquid looked and smelt nothing remotely like milk.

Janice, the unusually taciturn receptionist, offered a well-practised and, presumably, now perfected benevolent smile. "I do hope it's a false alarm. I'm so sorry," she repeated.

Chris suspected, due to the vast majority of the residents living in 'God's waiting room', Janice would revert to her sympathetic mode on occasions such as this. So, when faced with a relative of a resident who'd placed one foot from that metaphorical waiting room through to the other side, the well-trained receptionist knew to swap out her usual gossiping demeanour for something more befitting the situation. Despite her hopes, Janice knew, as did Chris and his sister, Jason Apsley was already some distance into that journey.

Janice glanced up from her computer screen, peering at him over the top of her glasses. Chris grabbed the well-chewed pen secured to the desk by way of a length of string pinned down by a hearty amount of gaffer tape. Usually, at this point in proceedings, Janice would launch into recounting the week's events thus far. This would include details about which resident had suffered a fall; bitching about another visiting relative's attire or lack of when describing the granddaughter of the woman in the next room to his father; how many residents had lost their false teeth or pissed themselves in the dayroom, or a combination of both, before rounding it all off with a moan about Miss Shrives, the manager, and specifically what a cow she was. However, today, Janice appeared to have put her inappropriate gossiping on hold, presumably recognising the pathos of the situation.

"I'm so sorry," she repeated for the third time.

"Thanks, Janice. I got here as quickly as I could. My sister, Beth, is chasing her way back from Cornwall."

"Oh, holiday? I wondered why I hadn't seen her this week."

"Yes, just a week away. I feel a wee bit guilty because I'm the one who encouraged her to go on holiday. As I said to Beth, we can't put our lives on hold on the off chance that Dad might take a turn for the worse," Chris replied after illegibly scribbling his name, date, and time.

Janice offered an agreeing nod and a slight shrug of her shoulders. Whether she agreed with what he'd said or not, Chris suspected it was just another expression she employed from her repertoire of sympathetic mannerisms when faced with this situation. She'd probably read one of the plethora of self-help books, this one specifically about how to appear genuine in a delicate situation when you don't actually give a toss. Although a long title, Chris was damn sure the paperback version existed somewhere on Amazon.

"I think the doctor's still with your father. I'll buzz you through."

Chris slid the book back across the desk as Janice pressed the door release buzzer to let him through from the reception area.

"Take care, Mr Apsley," she whispered.

Chris bounded towards his father's bedroom, the squawks emanating from his trainer's soles reverberating off the highly polished floor before echoing from the stark, hospital-styled corridor walls. Although not unpleasant, the waft of floor cleaner and disinfectant harboured an undeniable smell of impending death.

As Chris scooted around the corner, he suspected Janice would now be contacting the next in line on the waiting list to give them the good news that a room was about to become free. Although she and the staff were very caring, an empty room didn't pay their wages. Also, although said doctor was with his father, no pills or potions were available to cure dementia.

Chris slowed his pace as he approached when he noticed the door to his father's room stood ajar. Despite the almost deathly silence of the late afternoon, due to most residents taking up a spot in the day lounge whilst presumably trying to locate their lost dentures before their evening meal, Chris hovered by the door but couldn't detect the sound of any conversation. Then, fearing he was too late and his father had already left the 'waiting room', Chris tentatively stepped through to find who he presumed to be the doctor standing beside his father's bed. After a few seconds, taking in the scene, Chris cleared his throat.

"Oh, hello. Mr Apsley, I presume?" the doctor asked, as he spun around, portraying the same facial expression Janice had just offered. Either they'd both perfected it over the years or grabbed it on a two-for-one offer just for this moment.

The doctor's question was a reasonable assumption because the good doctor was presumably aware Chris had been summoned, probably at his suggestion. Following the doctor's rather formal greeting, Chris resisted the temptation to suggest he was Doctor Livingstone in reply. Anyway, apart from his sister, the likelihood of anyone else visiting his dying father was low.

Chris nodded a response, although focussed on his father as he lay in bed, eyes closed, mouth open, his skin appearing to have taken on a pale and pasty hue.

"Is …" Chris cleared his throat again, this time not to announce his arrival but to conjure up some saliva that seemed to have dried up at the sight of his father. "Has he gone?" he whispered.

"Oh, no. He's just resting. Stay with him, though. I've done all that I can." The doctor, a man Chris suspected to be ten years his senior, snatched up his bag of tricks from the bedside table before gently cupping Chris's elbow. "It's good that you're here. I'm afraid it won't be long now," delivered in that gracious tone, which Chris suspected the doctor regularly employed when on call-outs to the House of Death. Chris mused that if they paid doctors on the basis of piecework, the House of Death would be a nice little earner.

After offering a courteous nod, the bespectacled medic shimmied sideways and disappeared into that uninviting corridor.

Jason Apsley eased open an eye. "Has he gone?" he whispered.

"The doctor?"

Jason blinked, offering the tiniest of nods.

"Yeah," Chris nodded as he perched on the bed and took his father's hand. "Dad, it's me, Chris."

Jason blinked again but said nothing. Chris feared, as was an all too regular occurrence, his father had forgotten who he was.

"I know who you are, son. I'm not senile, even though I'm senile," he whispered, followed by a wheezy chuckle.

Chris offered a smile that he'd borrowed from Janice.

"Beth?"

"On her way. She's gone to Cornwall, remember?"

"What's in Cornwall?" Jason frowned and knitted his brows.

"Holiday ... she and Phil took Oliver with one of his school friends. She told you on Friday when she visited."

Jason nodded. "Son, I'm not going to be around much longer."

Rather than utter some old bollocks – a word his father had always favoured – like, 'Oh no, don't say that', Chris just nodded. Although Jason wasn't their biological father, he and Beth had enjoyed a close and honest relationship with their adopted parents. So, trotting out that 'everything was going to be alright' comment when it obviously wasn't didn't seem right. As his dying father had suggested, Chris knew time was a tad on the short side.

"Dad, what did the doctor say?"

"Not much. Apart from, did I want to see a priest?"

"Oh, really?"

Jason grinned. "I told him I don't believe in all that bollocks."

"I've no doubt you did," Chris snorted. Although he'd received that call from Miss Shrives, advising him that his father may not last the day, Chris allowed a moment of positivity to nudge in when noting that, unusually, his father appeared fully compos mentis. Perhaps that was his mind clearing as he prepared to leave the 'waiting room' – who knew? Certainly not the doctor.

"What time will Beth be here, d'you think?"

Chris checked his watch, not that he needed to, just that involuntary reaction to his father's question. He puffed out his cheeks and shrugged. "It'll be late. Not until this evening, I reckon. They have the M4 and M25 to negotiate, and you know what those two bloody roads are like. I tell you, last week I was stuck near Heathrow for that long, my mobile died and Megan thought I'd eloped with the woman from HR."

"Oh … what's she like?"

"Who?"

"The woman from HR."

"Oh … we don't actually have an HR department, as such," Chris chuckled. "It's just what I jokingly tell Megan I'll do if she insists on taking her mother with us on holiday. Never again, not after that Shirley-Valentine-type incident with the Greek waiter last summer."

"Ah … yes, I can imagine," wheezed Jason, appearing to stifle a laugh, presumably to avoid launching into a coughing fit. "Your grandmother, my mother-in-law, Frances, you remember her?"

"Course. Granny Fran."

"Yes, well, she would have run off with me if she'd had the chance. I think your mother knew as much, too."

Chris raised an eyebrow. Although Granny Fran had passed some years ago, Chris could remember she was like no other granny. Frances Lawrence epitomised the term *cougar*. That said, his father's mind was probably misremembering. Not wanting to sully the memory of his grandmother and keen to avoid slipping down that particular rabbit hole, Chris thought he'd change the subject.

"I'm sure Beth and Phil will do their level best to get here as soon as. Traffic jams and the inevitable contraflows aside, Beth will be demanding Phil sticks his foot to the floor."

Jason nodded. "Son, I need to talk to you about some … some things. I can't wait for Beth."

"Okay … but—"

"Don't tell me that I'll be okay until she gets here—"

"Dad—"

Jason raised his free hand, effectively halting what he presumed would be Chris's protests. "Son, just hear me out, okay?"

Chris took a deep breath, surprising himself at how shaky it appeared. These had been a super tough couple of years for his family. Just over a year had elapsed since their mother had passed after being diagnosed with stage three breast cancer and, soon after, their father was diagnosed with stage four dementia. No one had noticed his father's mental health decline, just putting his struggles with simple tasks down to being unable to come to terms with the loss of his wife. However, as much as he didn't want to believe it, he knew his father would not be around much longer. Maybe Beth would make it back in time, and perhaps she wouldn't – again, who knew?

"I need to tell you something."

Chris raised an expectant eyebrow.

"Son, I've wrangled over this decision for years. Up until this point, I've always concluded that it's best to let sleeping dogs lie. But … knowing my time is nearly up, and not really sure where I'll end up …" he momentarily paused, letting that odd statement hang in the air before continuing. "So, I think I should tell you. I'm aware this decision could be a huge mistake, but a man's future may well depend on what I'm about to say."

"Blimey, Dad. That all sounds a bit scary. What d'you mean, where you'll end up? Heaven doesn't exist, according to you."

"Ah, well, there could be somewhere else, and I don't mean down there with that red-faced chap sporting a set of horns."

"Dad, you're not making any sense."

Jason knew what he was about to say was far more ridiculous than the idea of the existence of the Devil or God. Unlike anyone in the land of the living who couldn't prove they'd seen those mythical beings, he, the previously dead Jason Apsley, was living proof of what he'd finally decided to disclose to his children.

Jason attempted to shift his withering frame on to his side, despite the considerable effort and discomfort this manoeuvre demanded. The good doctor had advised him that along with his failing mind, the rest of his organs also appeared to have decided to give up the ghost. Whilst accepting his son's help, as he struggled to perform what should be a straightforward task, Jason offered himself a wry smile for referring to the book of Genesis – the very publication he didn't believe in.

"Dad … I'm a bit lost. What are you talking about?"

"Please, Chris. Just hear me out."

"Okay … you're comfortable like that? On your side?"

Jason nodded, recovering his breath after his exertions.

"Right, come on then. Please don't tell me you're going to confess to a murder or an affair," Chris chuckled in an attempt to lighten the mood.

Jason coughed and glanced away. He'd never cheated on his wife. As for the other suggestion – no, he'd take that to his grave.

"Dad, you didn't? Haven't?" blurted Chris, a smidge concerned that no denial appeared forthcoming.

"Chris, you remember when you and Megan booked that holiday to … oh, bollocks, where was it?"

"New York?" interjected his son.

"No, but I'll come back to that one. I'm talking about that place out there somewhere in the east … in 2004."

"Oh, Phuket, Thailand."

"That's it."

"Yeah, how could I forget? You and Mum insisted we didn't go because you'd said about a friend who'd just returned from there and had mentioned how awful it was. I seem to recall that you paid for us to go to Hawaii. We'll not forget that in a hurry. That was a lucky escape … saved our lives, that did."

"It did."

"Anyway, what about it?"

"I'll come to that. Now, New York. Remember?"

"Christ, how could I not? I think you must have had a sixth sense. You bought us that excursion for us to visit Niagara Falls on the very day they hit the twin towers."

Jason nodded and grinned at Chris.

"Dad, have you got wind?"

"No, son. I'm just having a final moment to decide whether I'm actually going to go through with this."

"With what? And what's my holidays got to do with whatever you feel the need to confess?"

"They're examples of what I'm about to tell you."

Chris rubbed the back of his father's hand. Although an act of comfort, Chris wasn't sure if that was for himself or his father. "Go on … you have me intrigued."

"Okay, here goes. God help me."

"I thought you didn't believe … y'know, religion and all that bollocks."

"I don't, but someone … something is responsible."

Chris held his breath as his father cleared his throat, hesitating as if struggling to find the right words.

"I … or your mother, for that matter, don't … didn't possess a sixth sense, or exper … experyorsomething or other—"

"Extrasensory perception?"

"That's it. Frigging head is full of a load of mushy bollocks. No good my body parts going to medical science, my brain will yield as much information as a pink blancmange."

A moment of silence hovered between them. However, due to their close relationship, neither man felt awkward or compelled to fill the silent void.

"Son, where was I?"

"Recounting Megan's and my catalogue of near misses regarding our annual holidays and how you seem to have the ability to persuade me to go somewhere else just before some catastrophe occurs."

"Yeah, that was it. So, as I was saying, I knew that tsunami would hit Thailand on Boxing Day in 2004, and I also knew that terrorist attack was coming on nine-eleven."

Chris patted his hand and offered that Janice-type smile. Maybe with an unintentional patronising twist to it. Nevertheless, a humouring smile to the father he loved, whose mind had succumbed to a cruel disease – pink blancmange, to quote him.

Of course, his parents' lucky interventions regarding those two events saved Megan's and his lives. However, those were just coincidences – fortunate happenings that life often throws up. His father was the sort of chap that didn't believe in faith, religion, psychics, and horoscopes – all bollocks, according to him. Jason Apsley was no Danny Torrance. Nevertheless, Chris knew he had the propensity, a predilection if you like, to believe in determinism. His father's belief that small actions could prevent or cause unrelated consequences was probably why he subconsciously believed he could predict those events.

"Son, you haven't said anything."

"What, Dad?" Chris shrugged, inwardly disappointed that he seemed incapable of erasing the patronising twang to his smile, which he proffered to his dying father.

"Err … Son, did you hear me? I just told you I knew the future."

"Hmmm, yeah, I know."

Jason blew a short raspberry. "Christ, your mother always said you would be the hardest to convince. I said Beth would be. Maybe she was right. I knew I should have kept those damn exercise books."

"What books? Convince about what?"

"Look, I'll spell it out. This isn't going to be an easy listen, and I know you will dismiss what I have to say. I suspect you'll just put it down to my forgetfulness and the fact that I'm going gaga."

"Dad, you're getting all het up. What's this all about?"

"Listen." Jason wagged a finger to enforce his command. "In 2019, I died in a road traffic accident."

Chris patted his father's hand.

"Son, did you hear me?"

"Dad, it's 2016. You're not dead. You're here with me, remember?"

"No! Just listen to me," barked the dying man.

Chris knitted his brows. Even when suffering from this wicked disease, his father rarely raised his voice.

"After I died, I awoke in 1976 sitting in the driver's seat of my yellow Mark Three Cortina. Cockfosters High Street, just by the traffic lights next to Bejam's freezer centre. Well, it was then. Now it's one of those nail bars."

"Your Cortina? That classic heap of crap you insist I keep in the garage but never drive?"

"And you must never … never drive it!" boomed Jason, eyes bulging, before launching into a rasping coughing fit.

Chris grabbed the plastic cup of water from the bedside table and offered the straw to his father's lips.

Jason leaned forward and took a sip before flopping his head back onto the pillow. "Promise me. Promise me you will never drive that damn car."

"Alright."

"Promise!"

"Okay!" Chris shot his hands in the air. "I'll leave it exactly where it is, clogging up space next to my son's golf trolley, which he never uses."

"How is …"

"Jordan."

"That's him. My grandson behaving himself?"

"He's at university in Bath, remember?"

"Oh … is he that old already?"

"He is. They grow up fast, don't they?"

"Now, Chris. What about what I've just told you?"

"Ah … your secret, or confession. So, you didn't murder anyone; you didn't cheat on Mum; you time travelled. For a minute there, you had me worried this was going to be something serious," Chris chuckled, determined to keep the mood light. However, under that jocular demeanour lurked concern because his father's expression suggested he believed he was a time traveller. Chris mused that losing your mind had to be the worst of all the hideous medical conditions one could suffer from.

Jason raised his hand to point at Chris. "You've got it in one, my boy. Now, listen, this is important." Jason's grip on his son's hand became almost vice-like. "Chris, I've had forty-or-so years to think about this. I'm pretty certain that, when I die, a man with my name, who looks identical to me when I was forty-two, will time travel forward from 1976. Now, I need you to look out for him."

"Dad, you're gonna break my fingers if you're not careful."

"Chris," he hissed. "I was born in 1977. I time travelled from 2019 to 1976, where I took the place of a man who's also called Jason Apsley. He disappeared and, I suspect, will re-emerge when I die. You must look out for him."

Despite his frailty, Jason's grip on Chris's fingers caused them to become pale due to the constricted blood flow. As Chris attempted to break free from the vice-like grip, he felt an overwhelming feeling of loss of the father he loved.

"Dad, calm yourself. Come on. You're getting a bit muddled. You moved into that flat on the Broxworth when I lived with Carol. Although I can't remember much about that time or my biological mother, I do remember you were our neighbour before Carol died, before you and Mum adopted Beth and me."

"Son ... no! This man, *Other* Jason, as I call him. He moved there in the spring of '76 after returning from South Africa. I time travelled in August that year and took his place."

"Okay, okay," Chris stated, trying to calm him, desperately trying not to sound patronising. Although not wanting to play along, Chris needed his father to realise the ridiculousness of his rants. "And if that were true, what happened to this *other* Jason, then?"

Jason released his grip to fan out his hands whilst bulging his eyes as if playing the part of a wizard who'd just performed some stupefying magic. "He disappeared! Gone, vamoose. But this is it. When I'm gone, he will return."

Whilst allowing his poor deluded father to continue with his rant, Chris glazed over and became lost in his thoughts regarding the cruelty of the scene that played out before him. As ridiculous as his father's claims about time travel, it seemed as if some alien life force had taken his father's mind and replaced it with a pink blancmange.

Earlier this morning, after receiving that call from Miss Shrives, Chris had pelted across town. His Lewis Hamilton impression included breaking a few speed limits and nipping through a couple of amber traffic lights, all to ensure he didn't arrive too late to see his father. Although his father's heart was clearly still beating, Chris considered he'd arrived too late – Jason Apsley, his loving father, had completely lost his mind.

2

Blinded By The Light

The ominous reverberation of my skull cracking when thumping against the concrete step gave rise to suggesting that all was not good.

A moment before hearing that inauspicious sound, when blinded by the light of the low morning sun as it pierced the dark vista of the entrance to the stale-piss-stinking stairwell, my peripheral vision had momentarily spotted the arc of a sovereign gold ring before it and the fist it was attached to, slam into my face. Now, as I lie in that vestibule, which accessed the five levels of Belfast House, one of three grey monolithic concrete blocks that made up the odious Broxworth Estate, I considered that my time on this earth might have come to a rather abrupt end.

Bollocks – just when life was becoming interesting.

Precisely thirty seconds before this disagreeable altercation, some bastard in a Bedford van had rear-ended my car as I attempted to drive off the estate. The point at which I'd hopped out to give the driver of that crap heap of a van a mouthful was when the lights went out. The sheer ferocity of that punch sent me flying back into the stairwell that I'd scurried out of only ten minutes earlier when hurrying to get into town.

After fifteen years of living and working in South Africa, six months back in good-old Blighty and, despite temporarily renting a shithole of a flat on one of the country's most notorious estates, I'd stupidly allowed my guard to drop. When hopping out of my car to give that bloke what for, some lowlife scum had knocked me out. All of which had probably resulted in my untimely death.

And for what? My half-empty packet of Players? My wallet, containing a few pound notes, and keys to my second-hand yellow Cortina that now probably sported a crushed rear bumper and cracked tail light – not exactly a significant haul. But then, this was the Broxworth Estate – life was cheap.

There were two reasons for leaving my lucrative position as the principal mining engineer at one of the Southern Hemisphere's largest diamond mines. First, some months back, I'd come to accept that my time in South Africa had reached its natural conclusion. And second, I was kind of on the run, so to speak.

Now, just to be clear, no one, like the police, Interpol, or my previous employer's henchmen, were actively hunting me down. However, after leaving my employment with a bag of sparkly stones that weren't technically my property, and despite covering my tracks, there was always the possibility that they soon might be.

I guess it was reasonable to assume that my scuzzball attacker wasn't aware of the ill-gotten-gained contents of my safety deposit box – namely a handful of emerald-cut solid carbon – but just one of the many scumbags who regularly scouted the estate looking for an easy target to mug – like me.

Presumably, the rear-ending of my van was a joint setup with the driver and thug who'd rearranged my face. I'd heard muggings were becoming more refined than just a raised knee to the testicles.

In my haste to crack on with this morning's list of jobs, I'd allowed my guard to drop. I should have known better. Carjackings in my adopted country were commonplace. Just a few months back in a relatively peaceful Blighty I'd become complacent.

This morning I'd planned to sell a few of those purloined gemstones to a dodgy jeweller's even more dodgy contact. The former, a weasel of a man, who I'd made contact with last week. However, that meeting was now cancelled if I was about to leave this world after some douchebag sent their fist into the centre of my face.

The result of that altercation left me lying amongst the discarded chip paper, newspapers, and sweet wrappers, not to mention the pools of indeterminate liquids which afforded the stairwell that distinctive repugnant odour.

Two sets of black eyes peered at me as a couple of rats took a break from sniffing out their elevenses from the greasy morsels deposited in discarded chip paper. One of the sizable rodents nudged his nose into the wrapping, appearing to be the front page of last week's Sunday Express. The distinctive typeface just about decipherable in the unlit stairwell. The other one of my furry companions, which now seemed to have lost interest in the remnants of someone's fish supper, nudged a crumpled pack of Capstan cigarettes. A red, twenty-six-pence price label caught my eye. As I slipped out of consciousness, my brain tried to compute what that equated to in real money.

You see, for me, living abroad for so long, and despite the UK's conversion to a decimal currency just over five years ago, these new coins swilling about in my jeans pockets were still a bit of a head spinner. Just before my mind succumbed to the injuries sustained, I concluded it would be about five shillings and thruppence, give or take the odd ha'penny. Yes, that was far more straightforward than twenty-six pence.

"Oi, wanker. You ... move your friggin' arse," someone boomed in my face.

I'd never been one for attending church. However, on the insistence of my Presbyterian mother, I'd regularly attended Sunday school until the Luftwaffe dropped a hundred-pound bomb through the church roof in May of '41.

Fortunately for me, seven-year-old Jason Apsley, this event occurred on a Monday night, not Sunday morning, thus avoiding being blown to smithereens. Unfortunately, for him, a fate the creepy church warden didn't avoid. Rumours circulated among my mates that, as a result of the blast, the poor fellow's body parts were scattered over a vast area. One of my mates claimed to have found his watch in the neighbouring street. Anyway, assuming I was now dead, someone shouting 'oi wanker', despite my Sunday school teachings, wasn't how I presumed I would be greeted when approaching the Pearly Gates.

After my face suffered the tenderising effects of a ring-festooned fist and a fractured skull courtesy of that concrete step, I assumed that the most likely outcome was my death. Nevertheless, I cracked open one eye to assess who addressed me in this not-so-welcoming tone.

Fair to say, the scraggy woman who attempted to step around me didn't appear to be Saint Peter. Well, not that I knew what he looked like, but I'd be surprised if he was female and presumed he didn't usually wear what appeared to be tracksuit bottoms with the word 'Juicy' blazoned across the bottom. Also, based on my somewhat less-than-legal acquisition of a bag of diamonds, I didn't believe she gave a particularly accurate representation of the devil if that was where I'd ended up.

"Am I dead?" I muttered, somewhat surprised that, if I were, I would be able to suffer the mother-of-all headaches which now throbbed with the intensity of a beating djembe drum.

"Bleedin' will be if you don't get out the friggin' way, you twat."

"I beg your pardon." I lifted my head, my hand shooting up to the back of my skull to assess the damage caused by the altercation with that vicious edge of the concrete step.

"What you doing down there, anyway? You're liable to get mugged in this place, you twat," she bellowed whilst glaring down at me for blocking her path.

As I gawked up at her, I became captivated by the myriad of facial piercings that indiscriminately punctured various parts of her head. Either she'd lost a tussle with a rivet gun, or the girl must be one of those punks I'd read about and some shocking new band called the *Sex Pistols*. The arc of both ear helixes gave the appearance that a staple gun had shot off on some demented rampage.

Although I'd only lived on the estate for a few months, a temporary stopgap whilst searching and purchasing my new home, I knew most residents by sight. However, I didn't recognise this particular pugnacious woman who now glared down at me.

Despite her odd attire, my eyes were drawn to the repulsive collection of tattoos that liberally covered both arms poking out of the sleeves of a 'Rihanna Bad Girl' t-shirt. The Union-Jack-patterned-butterfly tattoo with *'made in 1996'* penned underneath in black ink was certainly the likes of which I'd never seen on a woman before. I presumed the *'1996'* part of her tattoo wasn't referring to the year of our Lord because that was twenty years in the future.

"I hit my head on that step," I muttered, checking for blood as I inspected my hand after gingerly rubbing my scalp.

"You shit-faced? Bit early for that, ain't it?"

"Sorry?"

"Pissed?"

"No. Some bastard larruped me one as I hopped out of my car. And can you please stop shouting?"

"Well, I ain't surprised you got mugged looking like that, you twat. This ain't a safe place to be wandering around, y'know."

"Like what?" I glanced at my t-shirt and leather jacket, wondering why she, of all people, could accuse me of appearing odd.

"Retro, like. All the hair and flares. You look like my granddad in those old pictures," she loudly announced before extracting a piece of white plastic from each ear.

The Broxworth Estate, although a clangourous crap-hole that never slept – a bit like New York, although I guess nothing like it – I struggled to see the need for wearing earplugs during the day. However, it answered the question as to why she felt the need to constantly shout.

"You the dippy twat who's parked his Beemer out there?" She thumbed over her shoulder in the direction of the community centre. "I'd get going before some tosser has it away with your alloys."

"Beemer? What's a Beemer? What are alloys?" I thought two questions were probably the limit for this woman to process, so I held back on why she constantly referred to me as a *twat*. Although I knew the meaning, twat wasn't generally used and certainly not uttered by a woman. Now, if she'd called me *spaz* or *mother fucker,* then, yes, they would be the usual derogatory put-downs I was more used to hearing.

"You for real? Your motor … your wheels. You said you just got out of a motor. Jesus, I reckon you did bang your head. I said some twat will make off with your alloys."

"Oh," I muttered whilst tentatively assessing the damage to the back of my head. "I think you must have me mixed up with someone else. The yellow Cortina is my car."

Although I had no idea what she was referring to regarding alloys, I certainly didn't need to worry about the hubcaps because they'd disappeared the first day I arrived in this odious place. With this in mind, as I peered through the gap to the roadway, it appeared stolen hubcaps were the least of my worries. The mugging team, comprising the driver of the Bedford van and his ring-festooned accomplice, appeared to have had it away with my car.

"Bleedin' hell, Cortina? What's that? You got one of those new electric motors, 'ave you?"

As I pulled my hand away from my scalp, I began to wonder if that crack on the head had affected my hearing. For one ridiculous moment, I thought she'd said electric car. Now, I knew the old boy along the landing zipped about the town in one of those Ministry-blue three-wheeler Invacars. However, that sported an air-cooled Villers engine, not powered by a battery.

The lack of fresh blood on my hand suggested the gash on the back of my head had stopped bleeding. However, despite deciding I wasn't dead, it became apparent that all was not well. Assuming, just for argument's sake, I was still alive after cracking my head on that step. There had to be a high possibility that I was now suffering from concussion and hallucinating.

However, leaving the state of my health to one side, when I'd zipped down those concrete stairs, what I presume was less than fifteen minutes ago, I'm reasonably confident that the walls weren't covered in graffiti. So, okay, not that I'd previously hovered to take in the ambience of the rat-infested stairwell but, somewhat oddly, the floor-to-ceiling splash of fading colours appeared to have been there for some time.

To add to this odd enigma, I noticed that my furry friends had scuttled away and that chip paper and the discarded packet of cigarettes were also missing. In their place was a collection of syringes nestled amongst a flyer advertising something called a Domino large pizza for fifteen pounds.

"Fifteen quid," I mumbled. "For a pizza?" Okay, so during the short period of time that I'd been back in the UK, I still performed those calculations when converting decimal currency into pounds, shillings, and pence. And, coupled with the fact that I was used to dealing in South African Rands, I'll attest that I struggled to convert the currency. However, irrespective of my lack of understanding of decimalisation, I was pretty confident fifteen quid could purchase either a weekly shop from Lipton's, two weeks of heavy drinking in the local, or a month's worth of cigarettes – not just a pizza.

"Oi, come on then. You're blocking the steps."

"Okay." I held my hand aloft as I shifted into a sitting position. "Rihanna, give me a hand … I'm feeling a bit groggy."

"Friggin' hell," she mumbled, shaking her head before stepping back. "I ain't that stupid, you twat. You'll try somefink."

"Try something?"

"Yeah, you one of those pervert types? This place is teaming with nonces."

"No. Course not. I'm not like that."

"Oh, well, you talk funny. I take it you ain't from around here."

Her retreat, prompted by fear I was about to do her some harm, indicated no hand of assistance would soon be forthcoming. "I've lived in South Africa for many years … I picked up some of the accent."

"Oh, what like that Olympic sprinter bloke with no legs who shot his girlfriend?"

"Sorry, did you say sprinter with no legs?" Christ, notwithstanding a bang on the head, I was clearly suffering from delusions.

"Yeah. Oh, and that Mandela bloke. Y'know, he was President of South Africa, wasn't he?"

"Nelson Mandela?

"Yeah, that's him."

"President?"

"Yeah, President or Prime Minister, or somefink or other."

Well, that confirmed it. This peculiar woman had to be some deranged lunatic who'd escaped from the mental hospital. If she wasn't, that could only mean I'd suffered severe brain damage as a result of my head colliding with that step. Whatever the explanation, there was no way a prisoner incarcerated on Robben Island had somehow escaped, joined the Soweto uprisings and overthrown the president, Nico Diederichs.

Whether that altercation with the ring-festooned thug had caused permanent damage to my brain, I thought I'd better see if I could stand. "Look, I live up on the second level ... flat 121." I nodded upwards whilst gingerly hauling myself into an upright position.

"Fuck off, do you. And anyway, who the fuck's Rihanna?"

As I slapped a hand on the graffiti-covered wall to steady myself, I noticed the woman sported a bolt through her tongue as she rolled around her chewing gum. During my time in South Africa and Southern Rhodesia, I'd become accustomed to many African tribes' cultures. Many of whom sported piercings and lip plates as an indication of wealth and social standing. However, never had I seen a white woman, albeit a scraggy one, with a piercing of this sort.

Whilst spitting out some blood, I wagged my finger at her t-shirt. "You ... Rihanna, that's your name, I take it?"

"You taking the piss? Rihanna! Y'know, hip hop ... Snoop Dogg, and all that."

"Jesus, what are you talking about? What's Snoopy got to do with your name?"

"You ain't right in the head, mate," she barked, whilst repeatedly tapping her index finger on her temple, pulling a gurning face, and offering up a vision of the Frankenstein-styled bolt that pierced her tongue.

Now mesmerised by her facial and mouth organ punctures, I just gawped back, unable to offer up any response. However, I venture to suggest she made a valid point regarding my mental well-being.

"I suggest you naff off, you twat. Oh shit, you ain't the feds, are you? No wonder some bastard stuck one on you."

"Feds?"

"Filth?"

"Sorry?"

"Fuck me! Old Bill, you twat."

"No, I just told you. I rent a flat up there," I thumbed up the stairs, indicating the second level. "Flat 121. I've been here six months or so."

"Oi, what's your bleedin' game? That's my flat, you twat."

"121?"

"You bleedin' deaf?"

"No. But I've got one hell of a headache, and you keeping on shouting ain't helping much," I barked, wagging my finger at her. "I may have banged my bonce, but I know where I live. Flat 121 is my gaff. I moved in the day the Brotherhood of Man won the Eurovision Song Contest in April."

Her jaw sagged.

I rolled my eyes. "Yeah, I know, shit song. I can remember the day I moved in because Carol from next door came around to introduce herself, saying that the UK had won. Not that it interested me, of course. I'm more of a Led Zep man myself."

"You need to get up A and E, mate."

"Sorry?"

"Bleedin' Led Zep? That shit my old granddad used to listen to about a hundred years ago. Fuck me. You need to get that head seen to."

"Sorry?"

"Led Zeppelin ... *Stairway to Heaven*. Mum had it played at his funeral when he died 'bout ten years ago. I was only ten, but I remember finkin' how shit it was."

Clearly, I was in the presence of probably the weirdest woman I'd ever met. And believe you me, I've met a few in my time. This conversation seemed to morph into something I might have experienced when smoking that pipe with the strange tobacco my roommate would regularly proffer during my university days. Anyway, despite my list of jobs planned for the day, I thought I'd better set this punk woman straight.

"You're mistaken, I'm afraid. Led Zep only released *Stairway to Heaven* a couple of years ago. Also, I doubt someone of your grandfather's generation would be interested in them. I imagine it would be more Gershwin and Al Johnson, or maybe a bit of Louis Armstrong."

"Wow ... you puttin' this on? I saw some bloke on YouTube who reckoned he'd come from the last century."

"You what?"

"Yeah, some dickhead who reckoned he's time travelled. The twat's got millions of followers who actually believe him."

"Followers?"

"YouTube … y'know, an influencer, who believes he's like that bloke in back to the whatever. Those old films from the '70s or whenever. My Dad loved 'em."

"Films?"

"Yeah, that flying car."

I shook my head, concerned that if I wasn't hallucinating, I was in the company of a tattooed lunatic. If I wasn't mistaken, she'd mentioned electric cars, and now ones that could fly, not to mention an Olympic athlete with no legs.

"Is this Candid Camera?"

"Do what? Candid what?"

"Oh, forget it. Whatever joke this is, I'm not interested." I attempted to push past her, intent on cracking on with my day.

"Go on, then, just for a laugh. What year d'you reckon this is, then?" she chuckled.

I exasperatedly shot my arms in the air. "Christ, I don't have time for this," I muttered, pushing past her into the central square after a couple of furtive glances left and right to ensure another douchebag wasn't waiting to have a second go.

"Well?" she called after me as I headed towards the community centre, specifically the alley that led off the estate. After being carjacked, I intended to find a bus stop because public transport was my only option to get into town.

I halted, turned around, and jabbed my finger back at her. "Look, love. I ain't got time for this. All that screaming and shouting and frankly obscene punk stuff you kids listen to these days is not only offensive, but it appears to be mushing your brains."

"Punk? Get that head seen to, you dippy twat!"

3

Downtown

"No mate. As I told you yesterday, and the day before, and all of last week, I ain't seen him, alright?"

Chris jabbed the photo he'd presented to the shopkeeper with his index finger, sliding it an inch or two further across the counter. "Just take another look … please." He surprised himself with how the last word uttered sounded to be in a pleading tone, considering the futility of his request.

The unkempt, bloated oaf, who Chris suspected rarely became acquainted with a shower or a toothbrush, took a hearty drag on his cigarette and exaggeratedly huffed before apathetically glancing at the photo. With one eye closed to avoid the smoke that drifted up his face, caused by the cigarette now firmly clamped between his lips, the fully paid-up member of the great unwashed shook his head.

"Nope, as I just said, never seen him." After removing his cigarette and noisily snorting back phlegm, he inserted his index finger in his left nostril before wincing when enjoying a frolicsome poke around the nasal cavity.

"Okay, thanks anyway," Chris offered with a shrug of his shoulders before reaching for the snap, only halting when the repulsive lump jabbed his snot-covered finger onto the picture. Chris scrunched his nose at the thought of what had just been deposited as he eyed the man's glistening wet digit.

"Anyway, mate, as I keep telling you, that photo was taken bleedin' years ago. If I ain't mistaken, that's one of those old Ford Cortinas that geezer is standing next to. Not that I ever saw it, way before my time, you see, but my uncle had one just like it."

"Yeah, I know."

"Oh, how did you know my uncle?"

"I didn't."

"You just said you did."

"No, I said I know that's a Cortina."

"Oh. Well, anyway, how the frig am I gonna recognise some bloke from a photo taken forty-odd years ago, then?"

"It's complicated," Chris replied, offering a tight smile. Before sliding the print back across the counter, Chris ensured he only touched the edge because he had no desire to catch whatever was causing the shop assistant to sniff repeatedly.

"Complicated? What d'you mean? That fella would probably be in his eighties by now. I'm hardly going to recognise him, am I?" he scoffed, offering a dismissive shake of his head.

"Look, the guy I'm trying to find is identical to the man in this photo." Chris nodded at the counter where he'd left the ancient snap whilst waiting for the great-unwashed's snot to dry. "He'd be a bloke in his early forties."

"Oh … what his son, or something."

"No … they," Chris hesitated. "They just look identical."

"Right … what, you some insurance investigator, are you? This bloke inherited a shitload of cash, and your job is to hunt him down, is that it?"

"Not really. It's a family matter."

"Oh, right. What like that show with Cilla? You're hunting some lost relative for some old crusty who's about to pop their clogs and want to see their long-lost sprog before they go."

"Cilla?"

"Yeah, you know that ginger Scouse bird who presented that show a few years back?"

"Blind Date?"

"No! Frigg sake. Y'know. Shit, what was it called when they searched for long-lost relatives? Christ, my brain can't remember anything these days."

"Ah, Surprise, Surprise, eh?"

"You what? What you saying?" he aggressively retorted, after firing out a stream of smoke from each nostril before continuing with his snorting bull demeanour. "Oi, pal, just because you got a whistle on, that don't make you any better than me, you pompous git."

"Excuse me—"

"Just 'cos I can't remember the name of the show, don't mean you can offer up your opinion, alright?" he barked, nudging his head forward. Either impersonating a chicken or feigning a head butt.

"I wasn't. I said, surprise, surprise … as in the show, *Surprise, Surprise*."

"Oh." His bottom lip sagged. Although it wasn't a good look, Chris thought the expression suited him.

"And no, I'm not part of some investigative team for any TV show, insurance company, or solicitors. I'm just trying to find this bloke who lived on the estate back in the '70s."

"Well, if he did, he ain't gonna look like that now, is he?"

Chris nodded, agreeing with the guy's assessment. Although his quest held a certain futility about it, he promised his father that he would try to find this man.

"Mum liked her, y'know. *Downtown*, she played it all the time."

"Sorry?" quizzed Chris, the repulsive shop assistant's statement hauling him from his musings.

"Cilla ... *Downtown*."

"That was Petula Clark. You're getting confused."

"Oh. You sure?"

"Yes, definitely. My mother had a pretty decent voice and used to sing it when doing the housework."

"If you say so, I'll bow to your greater knowledge. You should get yourself on Pop Master, mate."

"Excuse me?"

"On the radio. Pop quiz show."

"Oh ... sure." Chris glanced at the photo and winced, contemplating slotting it into his jacket pocket. "He's dead, but my father's convinced he would be living here," Chris muttered, more to himself than continuing the conversation.

"You've lost me, mate," he mumbled, before reinserting his finger into the other nasal cavity, burping, and snatching up his cigarette from the overflowing ashtray. Chris watched his swift, synchronised hand movements with disdain.

Although smoking in shops and public buildings had been banned for nearly ten years, the residents of the Broxworth Estate were selective regarding which laws they felt inclined to respect. In fact, due to the vast majority of those unfortunate enough to call this hellish dump home, most sporting criminal records of indeterminate lengths, the overwhelming majority regarded the laws of the land as guidelines rather than something that needed to be obeyed. Chris knew this better than anyone because the first six years of his life were spent living in one of these odious flats before his biological mother died of a drug overdose.

For as long as Chris cared to remember, the brutal grey concrete, sixties-styled monolithic hell-hole was a place to avoid. Even the authorities and the police tended to offer this diabolical cesspit a wide berth. So, the chances of a local police community support officer dealing with a misdemeanour like the flagrant violation of smoking laws was somewhere close to zero.

After inspecting the deposit stuck on the end of his finger and before scraping it down the side of his filthy-grey jogging bottoms, the unhelpful shop assistant aggressively poked his cigarette in Chris's direction. "So, you gonna buy something, then? This ain't the bleedin' tourist information centre or the National Archives. I've got a business to run, you know."

Chris offered a resigned nod. "Give us a scratch card, then."

"Is that it?"

"Yeah."

"Which one?"

"A winning one?" Chris offered with a smirk.

"Frigging comedian," he muttered whilst tearing off the card from the dispenser and slapping it on the counter. "Five quid."

"Five?" Chris blurted. "I usually only have one of the one-pound cards."

"You didn't stipulate which one. I've torn it off the strip now, so you're gonna have to buy it," he spat back, firing a blob of ash on top of the card as he jabbed his finger down to enforce his demands.

Chris offered a resigned shrug, relieved the deposit was only ash and not what was presumably now streaked down the man's joggers.

"Anyway, I should be charging you for information."

"You haven't given me any!"

"I told you the car is a Cortina and a rough guess of the age of the photo."

"I knew that already."

"Well, I didn't know that, did I?"

"Christ."

"Your problem, mate. Now, like every day this month so far, will you be back tomorrow asking the same question?"

"Yes ... probably."

"Okay. Well, to maintain the lifestyle I've become accustomed to ... " He paused whilst dramatically gesturing with his hand around the store, which Chris suspected was full of hooky gear, past its 'sell-by date' food, or both, before continuing. "So, from now on, I expect at least a ten quid purchase in exchange for information supplied." Again, he jabbed the cigarette at Chris to reinforce his point.

"Yeah, okay. Whatever."

Chris would not usually be of the mind to purchase a pointless gaming card. However, every day for the past two weeks, he thought he needed to buy something in return for picking the shopkeeper's brains. Nevertheless, he suspected the smelly git wouldn't tell him even if he had spotted the man depicted in the grainy snap because the Broxworth was just that type of place – no one stuck their head above the parapet around here.

Although, none too surprised that, once again, no one in the convenience store, Chinese takeaway or bookies recognised the man in the photo, Chris felt a pang of disappointment.

Chris hurriedly slotted the snap and scratch card into his jacket pocket before nodding a thank you to the repulsive oaf. For sure, parking a newish BMW on the Broxworth wasn't a particularly sensible idea. Keen to get back to it before the low-life piranhas stripped it clean, leaving him a shell of a car that would only be fit for the scrapyard, he hot-footed out of the store.

Although the stinking shopkeeper had stated that he'd never clapped eyes on the man in that photo, and based on the low probability of that man actually existing, Chris suspected the chances of locating the man were slim. No, scrub that, zero. Because the man depicted in that forty-year-old snap, plucked from his parent's photo album, was dead.

Chris, pleased that his car appeared not to have lost any wheels and all windows were still intact, so probably drivable, leaned up against the driver's door as he scratched the silver-covered boxes on the gaming card. Ten seconds later, he assessed the results after blowing away the foil scrapings. As were the previous fourteen he'd purchased over a two-week period, Chris wasn't overly surprised that today's purchase also appeared not to be a winner – not even a quid. He'd read somewhere that the odds of winning the jackpot on such cards were somewhere north of a hundred million to one, which was probably significantly better odds than locating the man who was dead.

After exchanging the pointless purchase for the photo from his pocket, Chris studied the image of his father. "Really, Dad?" he muttered. "How much longer do I need to keep up this charade?" he verbalised as if his dead father would answer. Chris absentmindedly rubbed the pad of his finger across the image, thinking about that surreal conversation they'd shared just over two weeks ago when his father had pretty much shattered his world with his deluded claims of time travel.

After nearly cracking his fingers, his father had rambled on with his absurd story about a man returning from the dead. Of course, Chris should have just put the ridiculous account down to the strange musings of a dying man. In an effort to stop his father's almost demonic rant, Chris had agreed to visit Cockfosters High Street and the Broxworth Estate every day for the first thirty days post his father's death.

Despite the utter futility of this pointless exercise, here he was now on day fifteen of this fool's errand. Namely, trying to locate a man who apparently had an identical name and appearance to his father and had been missing for forty years.

Of course, his father would never discover if he fulfilled that promise. However, he'd promised, and Chris harboured a strong sense of duty – a man of his word, you might say. And, despite knowing his quest to locate a forty-two-year-old dead man was pointless – yes, that's correct, he was searching for a doppelgänger for his father with the same name, who his dying eighty-two-year-old father reckoned died in 1976 – Chris would honour his commitment.

Total madness? Unquestionably. However, when thirty days of searching had elapsed, Chris's conscience would be clear. He would have fulfilled his promise to the loving man who'd raised him as his own.

The Broxworth Estate rarely benefited from any moments of serenity. The usual exchange of obscenities offered by residents and druggies who inhabited the burnt-out community centre provided a background hum that confirmed the pathos of the dire place. However, Chris became momentarily distracted from his father's picture by a none-too-civil-sounding verbal exchange between a man and a woman just in earshot.

"My good God," he muttered as he glanced up when spotting a man dressed in a tan leather jacket and retro flared jeans exiting the stairwell that served as access to Belfast House – one of the three tower blocks that made up the Broxworth Estate. Chris glanced down at the picture of his father, then back at the chap who'd swivelled around to shout at some woman at the foot of those concrete steps.

"No way. It can't be," he muttered.

4

Wish You Were Here

"Oh, bloody hell," I mumbled when stopping short of the community centre. Despite the disappearance of my car, which by its very absence suggested those bastards had nicked it, and placing my throbbing head and delusions to one side, there appeared to be something not quite right about the estate.

Well, yes, okay, there was a lot wrong with this place. But specifically, this morning, the odious estate appeared to have changed – still a dump, but a different kind of dump.

The three tower blocks, namely Belfast, Dublin and Shannon House, still stood in a circle where they had since the morons on the local council deemed it a good idea to build the estate fifteen years ago – sometime in the early '60s. However, nothing else appeared as it had last night.

Less than twelve hours ago, I'd staggered out of the community centre's bar after enjoying the darts match and at least four pints of Double Diamond and accompanying whisky chasers – enough for me to forget exactly how many. Now, in that relatively short period of time, the flat roof building, positioned in the central square, appeared to have taken on a full coat of graffiti.

Whilst trying to ignore the vacant stares from two hopheads slumped by the wall, my eyes were drawn to the now boarded-over windows and steel mesh fencing which guarded the door to either prevent entry or escape of whatever now behold there.

To add to this nuttiness, some bloke wearing a suit, leaning against a flashy-looking motor, appeared to be gawping at me as if I were some exotic caged animal. The safest policy around here was not to make eye contact with those you didn't know. As my nose and the back of my head could attest to, the estate was full of undesirables. Although this gaping-mouthed weirdo didn't appear to be your average estate thug, I thought it best to ignore him.

After receiving a ring-festooned fist in my face and some scrote pinching my motor, my planned day appeared to be turning to shit. Notwithstanding the odd appearance of the estate, with my planned meeting looming, I couldn't hang around to investigate. Time was now against me. I needed to pop into town, pick up that stash of diamonds, and meet up with that dodgy jeweller. The contact who'd offered to broker a deal with an even more dodgy dealer, who, for all concerned, remained nameless. Due to skirting rather close to those who operated well outside the law, not knowing the identity of my contact's contact seemed like a sensible precaution.

"Excuse me," called out the Suited-Gawper.

I glanced back in his direction before averting my eyes, somewhat surprised he was addressing me. Although his attire suggested he wasn't a resident, I became a smidge concerned by his official lilt. Considering my haul of ill-gotten diamonds, I feared he could be one of those who I felt sure would come looking for me at some point.

That said, I'd covered my tracks well, so I was probably being overly cautious. Assuming he was just a lost motorist and would at any moment ask for directions, I chose to ignore him and headed off in the opposite direction. Despite being more than capable of handling myself, when on the Broxworth Estate, it was prudent to be selective to whom you engaged with.

"Err ... excuse me."

Ignoring his repeated plea, I cracked on, heading for the bus stop on Coldhams Lane. Although that git had nicked my motor, the deal I would broker today could purchase fifty Cortinas. So, despite the inconvenience of having to use public transport, I wasn't overly concerned about the loss of my motor. In fact, I was more disappointed to lose my collection of cassette tapes, especially *Pink Floyd's Wish You Were Here,* which I'd recently purchased from Woolworths.

Once I'd completed my meet with said dodgy jeweller, I'd report the theft for insurance purposes. Presumably, sometime later this morning, after some scumbag had used my car in a robbery, it would be burnt out on some piece of waste ground or sold on with a set of false plates attached.

"Bollocks," I muttered, before halting my zip across the central square after patting my jacket pockets and realising that I'd left my cigarettes in the flat. Not keen on traipsing back up to Belfast House and presuming the Suited-Gawper would have found someone else to wave his A-to-Z at, I headed over to the newsagents-cum-local store.

Similar to how the community centre appeared to have miraculously altered its appearance, I was somewhat surprised to see that the newsagents had morphed its front façade from Wavy Line Central Stores to T–wats Convenience Store. That said, the piece of signage between the *T* and *wats* appeared to be missing. So, I presumed the owners were in the process of erecting the new signage and not naming it after that tattooed girl's favourite word.

In my peripheral vision, I detected the suited guy heading towards me. Clearly, he was persistent. "Sorry, pal, I'm new around here. I suggest you ask someone else for directions," I called out as I grabbed the shop's door handle.

Despite the small Hertfordshire town being my birthplace, and up until attending university I'd called Fairfield my hometown, I wasn't technically lying after living for fifteen years in South Africa.

"My, God. You look just like him," he exclaimed.

"You what?" I spat back. "Look, pal, I'm in a bit of a hurry." I yanked open the door and barrelled into the store, only halting my advance to the counter when noticing its absence. Not only had Old Harry, the shopkeeper, changed the name of the place, but somehow he'd managed to completely alter the internal layout within the space of a few short hours.

Whilst hovering a yard inside the door, the Suited-Gawper entered and stood by the entrance, doing what he did best – gawping open-mouthed in my direction.

"Is there something wrong with you?" I barked, eyeing him up and down. Although his stupid facial expression was starting to grate, my frustration was probably more born out of trying to understand why everywhere appeared, well, different.

"You're not by any chance called Jason Apsley, are you?"

When fronting him up, he stepped back a pace. I presumed an involuntary reaction when detecting my demeanour wasn't overly affable. "Who's asking?" I barked, raising an eyebrow.

"Oh …"

Although not a difficult question, Suited-Gawper appeared stumped for an answer. "Well?"

"You first."

"Me first, what?"

"Your name. Are you Jason Apsley?"

"Look, mate. I asked you who you are."

Apart from the Broxworth being the sort of place to avoid confrontation, years of living in South Africa had taught me to keep my guard up. So, it's a pity I'd forgotten that when hopping out of my car. Then, I might not be suffering from a mother of all headaches and could avoid using the bus.

"Chris. I'm Chris."

"Okay, Chris. So, why are you following me, and why do you want to know who I am?"

"I think my father knew you. Well, no, that's not strictly true because he never met you, if you see what I mean?" The last part of that sentence trailing off as he presumably realised the ridiculousness of the statement.

"He did, or he didn't?" I probed, whilst assessing the threat he posed. A man of similar age, roughly the same height, but sporting a bit of a paunch. However, the aura he gave off suggested he'd keep his fists away from my already bruised nose. Also, despite the suit, his questioning style indicated he wasn't the Old Bill.

"It's kinda complicated ... but my father said you would be here. Although, to be honest with you, I didn't really believe him. So, I take it you are Jason Apsley, then?"

"Yes, pal. And without appearing overly rude, what the hell has that got to do with you?" As I threw out my question, my eyes were drawn downward to the photo clamped in his hands.

Chris, noticing where my line of sight had drifted to, flipped around the picture and held it aloft. "Is this you?"

I snatched it from him. Although not needing to take a closer look because it was clearly a picture of me perched on the bonnet of my now missing Cortina, I couldn't recall when or where the photo had been taken. Or by whom, for that matter.

As I studied the picture, I wondered if I was suffering from some sort of concussion. Less than six months had passed since returning to the UK, and I was fairly certain I couldn't recall ever posing for a photo, which this picture suggested I had.

"Where the hell did you ..." my question trailed away as I flipped the picture over and spotted my handwriting on the reverse.

Me and that yellow Cortina — January 1977

"Jason?"

I glanced up from those written words, which I'd penned, but hadn't. "I don't understand," I muttered.

"You are Jason Apsley, and you were born on the 30th of March 1934?"

I narrowed my eyes at him. Despite deciding he wasn't the Old Bill, his knowledge concerned me. Of course, I could have bluffed it out, not offered any information, purchased some cigarettes and got on with my day, which would be the sensible option. However, far too many odd things were afoot, and I needed some answers.

"Jason, what year do you believe it to be?"

"Why does everyone keep asking me that question?" I mumbled, thinking about the tattooed girl and the peculiar things she'd earlier uttered. Notwithstanding the oddities of the last half hour, post receiving that nose realignment, there was clearly a problem. Today was the 12th of August 1976. Somehow, I'd written on the back of a photo, which I don't recall being taken, 1977.

"The year?" he raised an eyebrow at me.

"If you don't know, then I suggest you're a spazo like that tattooed girl."

"No, I know what year it is. But I'm asking you. What year do *you* think it is?"

"Christ, this bloody estate," I mumbled before slapping the snap on his chest and pushing past him as I bounded towards the counter. Whatever was afoot, my throbbing brain was in dire need of nicotine.

"Where's Harry this morning?" I asked the unshaven oaf slumped on a stool thumbing through a girlie mag. "What's with the screen, then?" I tapped the plastic shield, the sort you'd find in banks and some post offices were installing.

"Ah, I see he's found you then."

"You what, mate?"

The unshaven lump pointed his cigarette towards Chris. "He's been trying to track you down for weeks. I said I see he's found you. Get a hearing aid if you can't hear me."

Ignoring this new shop assistant's rude putdown, I glanced back at Chris, who remained in position whilst holding that photo slapped to his chest. It was reasonable to assume the nutter fully intended to continue our conversation. However, based on the fact he'd been hunting for a couple of weeks, I thought I better prize some answers out of him after grabbing a packet of cigarettes.

"Where's the fags?" I glanced past the rude git, more than a smidge bemused when faced with what appeared to be a set of sliding doors instead of the cigarette counter.

Old Harry's replacement slid the door back. "Which ones?"

"Oh … twenty Number Six."

"Do what?"

"Player's Number Six."

"Christ, you taking the piss?"

"Sorry?"

"Frig me. My old gramps used to smoke those," he chuckled. "I don't know if you can still buy them."

"Err … I bought a packet yesterday."

"Not from here, you didn't, mate."

"I did … oh, Jesus, give us a pack of Embassy, then," I huffed, frustrated by how difficult it seemed to have become to purchase a packet of cigarettes.

"Which ones? Gold, Silver, Superkings?"

"Number One."

The unshaven oaf allowed the door to slide back before turning on me from behind his protective screen. "Look, mate. I don't know what you're up to. But I'm just sitting here enjoying a good gawp at the lovely Cassy's tits," he tapped his finger on the glossy picture of a naked young lass in his mucky mag before continuing. "And you trotting out names of discontinued brands of cigarettes is starting to get on *my* tits."

I noticed Chris had joined me at the counter, slowly shaking his head from side to side whilst still managing to offer that odd, mesmerised, gawping look he appeared to prefer.

Due to my brain receptors demanding nicotine, I held my hands aloft in a placating manner. "Any packet of Embassy cigarettes."

After offering an exaggerated tut and sliding back the doors, he slapped the packet on the counter. "Thirteen-sixty-five," he announced, keeping his hand on top of the packet, thus preventing me from grabbing it from the serving hatch.

"You what?"

"You want them?"

"Sorry, mate. Did you say thirteen quid?" I exclaimed, concerned that if he had, I required a hearing aid as he'd earlier suggested.

"I'll get them," Chris interjected, waving his credit card before tapping it on top of what appeared to be a calculator perched on a metal arm. After two short beeps, the shopkeeper handed me a green-coloured packet. The wording suggested they were Embassy Cigarettes. However, I mused that the picture of a grave depicted on the front of the box to be an odd rebranding choice to replace the red flash across a white background.

"Jason, if I'm correct in what I'm thinking has happened, although I have no idea how it could. I mean, it's frigging nuts. But listen, you're going to need my help."

After tearing away the plastic wrapping and flipping up the lid, I glanced at him. "What did you say your name was?"

"Chris," he held out his hand. "Chris Apsley."

"Apsley?" I muttered. "Have we met before?"

"Yeah … yeah, we probably have. Although I was only about five or six, I seem to remember you moving next door when I lived with my mum, Carol.

After extracting a cigarette and popping it between my lips whilst maintaining eye contact with the man with the same surname, I patted my pockets, searching for my matches.

"Give us one of your cheap lighters, mate," Chris called out to the shop assistant, who'd returned to enjoying the visual delights Cassy had to offer. Chris again tapped his credit card on that calculator and handed me the lighter before grabbing my arm and hauling me away from the counter. "Let's go outside. You can't smoke in here."

"Who said?"

"The law."

I narrowed my eyes, taking the cigarette from my lips. Although fully aware you wouldn't generally light up in a food shop, I wasn't aware of a law that covered places such as the local newsagents on a shitty estate. Anyway, that moron hiding behind that security screen who'd replaced Old Harry appeared quite content to puff away on his cigarette whilst gawping at his mucky mag.

"Look, Jason, let's go outside."

"Hang on, are you saying we used to live next door to each other?"

"Yes."

"When?"

"About forty years ago … 1976."

5

Thrilla in Manila

"Oi. You wanna watch this one. He's a bleedin' headcase," squawked the Tattoo-Girl as she pushed past Chris and me as we exited the newsagents.

I scowled back at her but offered no response, focusing all my efforts on lighting a cigarette.

"Jason," Chris grabbed my arm again, encouraging me to walk with him.

"Hang on," I somewhat belligerently blurted before exhaling a plume of smoke through my nostrils. Although the nicotine rush satisfied my brain, it did nothing to explain how the estate had morphed its appearance. "You say your name is Apsley ... the same as mine?"

Chris halted, although still with his hand cupped around my leather-jacket-clad elbow. "Correct."

I took another drag of my cigarette before glancing at his hand, suggesting he should remove it. "And, d'you want to explain to me how you know my date of birth?"

"It's my father's date of birth. Well, one of them," he chuckled.

"You've got two fathers?"

"No. Well, yes, but no. I never knew my biological father. But I'm discovering that my adopted father had two birthdays."

"What, like the Queen?" I replied with more than a hint of sarcasm. "What, is he some toff who also gets an official birthday?"

"No … you see, I'm starting to come around to the idea that he was born twice. Both times on the 30th March, but forty-three years apart, if you get my drift?"

"You're not making any sense."

"I know," he nodded, "But please, hear me out. My father—"

"And who is he, exactly?" I interrupted.

"He was Jason Apsley."

"Was?"

"Yeah, he passed away two weeks yesterday."

"Were we related?" As soon as I'd asked, I knew the pointlessness of the question. Although I'd never delved into my ancestry, I was reasonably confident no other Jason Apsley existed in the family tree.

"Good question," he chuckled. "This is utter nuts, you know."

"What is?"

"You!" he exclaimed, grinning and waving a digit at me. "Although my dad believed in your existence, I thought he was losing his mind."

"What the hell are you rambling on about? You're not making any sense, pal." I jabbed my cigarette at him. "And was this packet of fags really thirteen quid?"

Chris smirked. "How much did you pay for your last packet?"

"Jesus, will you start answering some questions?"

Chris raised an eyebrow whilst still sporting that rather annoying stupid grin.

"Oh, okay, whatever. I think the pack I bought yesterday was five shillings ... which is about twenty-five pence, isn't it? I still can't get my head around this new money."

"Fuck me!"

"No thanks, mate. Anyway, I know the country's in a bit of a mess, and inflation is running riot, but I can't see how a packet of fags could have hit ... well, thousands of per cent inflation since yesterday. Bloody hell, even South Africa, with all its economic problems, hasn't hit those sorts of numbers. Jesus, man, even Big Jim, with all his cock-ups, couldn't have caused that sort of economic meltdown."

"Big Jim?"

"Callaghan."

"Who?"

"The Prime Minister, you spazo. What the hell has happened overnight? Fags now cost an average man's daily wage, and the community centre seems to be boarded up," I jabbed my cigarette at the two hop-heads who remained slumped against the wall, vacantly taking in our conversation. "Old Harry's newsagents has not only changed its damn name but gone through some dramatic transformation," I jabbed my thumb over my shoulder to what should be the Wavy Line Store. "And, some bastards nicked my Cortina—"

"The yellow one?" Chris interrupted. "As in that photo?"

"Yeah. And how come it's got 1977 written on the bloody back? I know I never—"

Chris held his hand aloft, indicating I should halt my rant. "Jason, what do you think the date is today?"

"That again. Christ, man, don't you know?"

Chris widened his palms and raised his eyebrows.

I huffed. "12th of August 1976."

Chris tipped his head back as if Ali had just landed an uppercut-right hook combination, similar to when pounding Joe Frazier last October.

"Fuck me! It's actually true!" he announced to the cloudless sky.

Whilst Chris exclaimed whatever revelation was true to whoever in the sky, I took a hearty drag on my cigarette, contemplating it was probably time to leave this nutter to his strange musing and make my way into town. Although I wasn't of a mind to pay the average weekly wage for a packet of cigarettes, if that's what actually happened back in T-wats newsagents, I reached for my wallet to offer him a couple of quid.

"Shit! That bastard mugged me. He had it away with my wallet," I blurted whilst feverously searching my pockets.

"Mugged?" Chris asked, recovering from his Ali-uppercut pose.

"Yeah," I mumbled, my cigarette bouncing between my swollen lips. I removed it after giving up on my pocket-patting routine and waved my hand towards the stairwell before continuing. "Some scuzzball mugged me after some bastard rear-ended me in a shit-heap of an old Bedford van. When I hopped out to assess the damage, the douchebag knocked me clean out. I ended up in the entrance to the stairwell, and the shithead made off with my motor."

"Jason ... before you were mugged, you were driving your car. The yellow Cortina, yes?"

"Don't you listen. I hopped out and got mugged."

"And at that point, it was 1976, yes?"

"What d'you mean, *was*? Course it's '76!"

Chris appeared excited as he stepped towards me. "Look, you say he knocked you out. So you were unconscious, yeah?"

"What is this? You're not the Old Bill, are you?"

"No. Listen. Did you hurt yourself ... you know when you were mugged?"

I pointed to my now swollen lip. "Yeah, the douchebag gave me a fat lip, and I cracked my skull on the concrete step."

"Fantastic!"

"You for real? I've got a bleeding great gash on the back of my head. What the hell is fantastic about that?" I fired back, whilst rubbing my dried-blood-matted-hair scalp, wincing at the touch.

Chris, still sporting that smirk with bulging eyes, giving off that Marty Feldman look, raised his palms. "Jason, I think you're dead."

With that misaligned-bulging-eyes look of that comedy actor lodged in my mind and his connection to Tim Brooke-

Taylor in the *At Last the 1948 Show*, I wondered if this was some surreal sketch from *The Goodies*. I glanced up, half expecting them to appear on their 'trandem' bike dressed in Union Jack waistcoats.

Whilst allowing the smoke to drift from my mouth, I shook my head and stepped back a pace. "You're a lunatic. My God, I haven't got time for this." I backed up a couple more paces, keen to insert some distance between us before hightailing back to my flat to grab some cash and finally crack on with my day. Unfortunately, my dodgy jeweller wasn't the sort of chap to be kept waiting.

Chris stepped towards me. "I'm so sorry, Jason. But I'm pretty sure you died when you hit your head."

"Whatever you've been smoking, mate, you need to lay off it for a bit." I'd heard reports that marijuana, previously a drug preferred by hippies, was becoming more mainstream and now the drug of choice for young professionals. This Chris bloke, with the same surname as me, appeared to be a habitual user. I spun on my heels and marched away towards the stairwell.

"Jason," he called out as I increased the distance between us.

I offered the reversed Churchill salute over my shoulder as I hot-footed away.

"Jason … Jason, hold up."

I could hear his footsteps gaining on me. Rather than attempt to outrun this idiot, I turned and jabbed my cigarette at him. "Naff off!"

"Jason. I'm sorry, mate. Unfortunately, you died the same day as my father, albeit forty-three years apart … the 12th of August."

Despite my urge to get away from him, I felt compelled to offer some verbal abuse – anything to get rid of the nutter. "Christ, man. Just naff off and leave me alone. Whatever deluded sludge is rolling around that head of yours, I'm not interested in hearing about it. Now, piss off."

As I took another drag of my cigarette, I mellowed when remembering this stranger had purchased the packet.

"Thanks for the fags. If you stick your address through my letter box, I'll send you a postal order to cover the cost."

Chris opened his mouth to speak, but I raised my palm to stop him.

"Look, I haven't got time for all this. You're clearly deluded. A minute ago, you said your father died a couple of weeks back. Now you're saying he died today."

"My father died twice."

I shook my head and performed a double-take as my jaw sagged, not in surprise at this continued lunacy but more in disappointment at his persistence.

"My father, Jason Apsley, died on the 12th of August 2019, and then again two weeks ago."

"Bloody hell," I snorted. "You poor sod. Now, look, I'm sorry that you're suffering from whatever delusions have got hold of you, but I have an urgent appointment to keep."

"In 1976?"

"Oh, piss off."

Chris grabbed my jacket, hauling me back before hopping backwards when I raised my fist. Not that I was in the Muhammad Ali league, but, as I said, I could handle myself. I presume Chris realised that when releasing his hand from my jacket and stepping back to avoid my poised and primed southpaw.

"Before you punch me, take a look around you. Does this look like 1976?"

The nutter made a good point.

Since exiting the stairwell less than half an hour ago, I'd been struggling to understand how the estate could have dramatically changed in less than twelve hours. I opened my fist to indicate I no longer intended to thump him. "What happened to the community centre?"

Chris glanced around at the derelict building, which had been packed with drinkers last night. "I was only about ten when it happened, and by then, I wasn't living here. I think it happened around the time of the Brixton riots. That would be in 1981, there, or thereabouts. Half the estate figured they'd jump on the bandwagon and trash the place, setting it on fire. The council refused to repair it, so they just boarded it up. It's full of crackheads now."

"1981?"

Chris turned around, offering me an affable smile, his eyes appearing to radiate pity. "Jason, as much as it is totally ridiculous, like my father, who apparently died in 2019, you've time travelled."

I wagged my index finger at him. "Please, just go away and return to whatever loony bin you've just escaped from." I spun on my heels and bolted up the stairs, simultaneously pinging my cigarette butt to join that collection of needles before grabbing the packet and lighter from my jacket pocket. Not that I would generally chain smoke, but I felt the need for another.

Regardless of the nutter's musings, there was no denying that the community centre had transformed its appearance. Not to mention Old Harry's shop, Tattoos-Girl's claim that Led Zep recorded *Stairway to Heaven* in the last century, and apparently ten packets of fags now cost the same as a portable TV, the likes of which I'd just splashed out on when perusing the offer in Rumbelows in the High Street.

At a little over one-hundred-and-fifty quid, that TV I'd purchased was pricey enough. I recall the sales assistant encouraging me to splash out on a massive twenty-six-inch Pye colour TV, presented in a fetching walnut surround. However, it was twice the price, and I couldn't see the need for a colour TV.

The electronics whizz-kid, who could only have been in his early to mid-twenties, then proceeded to bore the pants off me when relating a story about an American manufacturer who'd developed a television remote control unit. According to him, this company based their idea, which would allow you to change channels on your TV without having to touch the TV itself, on similar pieces of kit the bomb disposal boys were now using to deal with car bombs in Northern Ireland, which I believed was affectionately known as the *'Wheelbarrow'*.

Anyway, when I'd glazed over whilst penning a cheque to cover the purchase of my more than adequate black-and-white TV, the enthusiastic lad rabbitted on about the new *Pong* video console game, which he predicted would sweep the nation. Despite his enthusiasm, I'd politely informed the fresh-faced chap I doubted there would ever be a market for a remote-controlled television or an electronic game, for that matter.

Whilst musing about the apparent supersonic rise of inflation, I halted at my front door and searched my pockets for my keys. "Shit," I muttered, when realising my keys were hanging in the ignition of my car and everything that I'd left the flat with had been nicked by that ring-fisted git who mugged me.

Despite being unable to gain entry to my flat, that was not my only concern. Placing Chris's ridiculous suggestion that I was some version of a real-life Doctor Who on one side, there was irrefutable evidence that all was not right. Either that crack on my head had left me in a state of permanent delusion, or my flat had acquired a new front door since slamming it shut less than half an hour ago.

Fortunately, the old gent next door, Don, held my spare key for just such an eventuality. Knowing the old First World War veteran rarely ventured out, I tapped on his kitchen window. "Don. Don, you in there?"

The kitchen window flew open. "Piss off, I ain't buying whatever shit you're selling," an elderly woman barked, holding the window handle whilst pulling a gurning face.

"Oh … sorry, is Don there?"

"Don, who? You've got the wrong flat. There's no Don here," delivered in the same pugnacious tone before pulling the window in.

"Jason."

As I glanced around, I spotted Chris heading my way. To add to my crazy morning, it appeared I'd gained a lunatic stalker.

"What now?" I whined, raising my hands. "Can't you just leave me alone?"

"Jason. Don lived there in the '70s. Unfortunately, he died thirty years ago. I'm sorry, mate, but this is 2016."

6

Sputnik

I groaned in despair as I gently rested my forehead on the wall between mine and Don's flats. "Christ, why today?" I muttered, as my new stalker made up ground along the landing. As he approached, I called out to him whilst keeping my forehead planted firmly on the brickwork. "I don't suppose you could drop me in town. I have an appointment, and I seem to have also lost my keys."

Although not wishing to spend any more time in his company, I considered he could be my only remaining option to ensure I made it to that meeting with a couple of unscrupulous jewellers. Despite presuming the bus fare would only be about thruppence-ha'penny, without gaining entry into my flat, even that amount was beyond me. Along with everything else, it appeared my mugger had also nabbed all my loose change.

Chris, still advancing, didn't answer. Instead, choosing to focus on avoiding Tattoo-Girl, who zipped along in his slipstream before bustling past and halting at my flat. As she rammed the key into the lock, she glared at me.

"What you doing here, you weirdo?"

That was it – I'd had enough. "Me!" I exclaimed, turning on her. "I'm not the one looking like a tattooed witch with enough facial perforations to turn your head into a colander. With that amount of metal sticking out of your head, I'd steer clear of any magnets if I were you. Christ Almighty, how the hell, looking like that, can you have the bloody gall to call me a weirdo? And … and why are you trying to gain entry to my flat?"

"You what? Piss off, you twat. As I told you earlier. This is my flat."

"It's my flat!" I exclaimed, slapping my hand on the black-painted door, which earlier today was red. In the back of my mind, I noted that the paint was dry, so it couldn't have been painted whilst this morning's events unfolded.

"Jason." My stalker grabbed my arm, which I aggressively shook off.

"Get off me. What's the matter with you? You're not one of those poofter blokes, are you?"

"If this prick is wiv you, I suggest you have a word 'cos my Grant will be back any minute now, and he's the sort to throw a headbutt then ask questions." She barked, feigning a headbutt as if to demonstrate the technique.

"Sorry. He won't bother you anymore."

"Bleedin' think not. Brotherhood of Man, for fuck sake," she muttered, shaking her head at me as if *I* was the nutter here.

"Hang on," I barked, keeping my hand on the door, effectively barring entry and blocking her from turning the key. "That's my flat. I don't know how you've got hold of my keys, but you're not going in there."

"May I?" Chris nodded to the newspaper she clutched along with a box that stated it contained soya milk, which I very much doubted because the cardboard would be soggy. Anyway, what the hell was soya?

"Oi, that's my Grant's paper," she spat, slapping away Chris's outstretched arm.

"If I can just show the front page to Jason, I promise he will leave you alone."

"What's on the front page?" I furrowed my brows, now playing head tennis between Tattoo-Girl and my suited stalker.

"Yeah, whatever," she nonchalantly replied whilst handing the paper to Chris. "If both of you value your bollocks, you better bounce before Grant gets back. He's well dench, and it don't take much to get him vexed. Nuttin he likes better than an excuse to nut someone."

Bewildered, I shook my head at her. Although I'd spent a significant chunk of time abroad, so missed out on a few cultural changes, I struggled to understand most of what she just said. However, I gathered that her fella must be some big chap with a penchant for violence.

"Jason, look."

I glanced up at the redtop newspaper, which he held aloft. "What the hell am I supposed to be looking at?" I huffed in frustration.

"Jason, look," Chris tapped the page, raising his eyebrows and smirking.

I scanned the picture and headlines of some woman called May, who stated she would commit to the result of the referendum, repeating her mantra that *Brexit means Brexit.*

"Sorry, I don't know who that is or what this Brexit thing is either."

"Not the headlines, the date."

"Who's this May woman?" I asked, ignoring his request.

"The Prime Minister, but—"

"What happened to Big Jim?"

"Jason, that's irrelevant. Look at the date."

"No. You tell me what's happened to Callaghan."

"Who the frig's Callaghan?" blurted Tattoo-Girl.

"The bloody Prime Minister. Well, he was yesterday. What's happened to him?"

"Jason, I would expect the bloke's dead."

"Really? When did this happen?"

"Oi, give us me paper," she held out her hand, which Chris batted away. "Oi!"

"Hang on," he hissed at her.

"Your bleedin' funeral."

"What the hell is going on? I saw Callaghan on the news last night. He can't be dead."

"Christ, just listen. This is what I'm trying to tell you. I'm pretty sure the bloke is dead. If not, he'll be over a hundred by now. Look at the damn date, man."

"What's this got to do with her trying to bust into my flat?"

"Oi, it's my flat, you twat."

Chris nodded at Tattoo-Girl. "Hang on." When turning to me, he again tapped the paper. "Jason, for the love of God, please read the damn date."

I can't be certain how many times my eyes flitted across the date stamp, but I guess it was somewhere north of ten before Tattoo-Girl snatched the paper from Chris's grasp, pushed past me and scurried into my flat. After muttering a string of obscenities, she slammed the door, leaving me staring vacantly across the central square at Dublin House – the equally odious tower block facing the one I called my temporary home. I side-eyed Chris, who maintained that raised eyebrow expression.

Throughout my life, I'd occasionally landed in the odd spot of bother. However, situations were usually manageable, and with careful planning and level-headedness, there was always a solution to any difficult situation. Also, I was sensible, well-educated with a Batchelor of Arts degree and a teaching qualification to my name. Before I'd syphoned off my nest egg, that bag of hard-carbon stashed in my safety deposit box, I'd led a team of engineers in the challenging and sometimes dangerous mining industry.

I was nobody's fool.

However, after that faceless thug had rammed his fist into my face, all appeared not to be well with the world. At this point, I felt the need to triage my situation down to a more manageable size because trying to rationalise the last half-hour's events could lead me to a padded cell. Despite my flat no longer appearing to be my flat, and the sensible option would be to gain entry and throw that Tattoo-Girl out, I thought I'd deal with what was right in front of me.

"Who are you again?"

"Chris Apsley. As I said earlier, we met about forty years ago when I was about five or six."

"When I was about the same age? During the Blitz?"

"No. You were the age you are now ... forty-two, correct?"

I nodded, fumbling for my packet of cigarettes.

"Flat 120," Chris paused as he nodded along the landing. "I'm guessing you think Carol Hall and her little lad live there?"

I nodded whilst lighting the cigarette.

"D'you remember the boy ... Carol's boy?"

"Yeah. Little weedy lad. I feel sorry for him. I'm not talking out of turn, but Carol won't win any Mother of the Year awards anytime soon."

"And that boy's name."

"Oh, err ... Christopher, I think."

My suited stalker nodded and poked his chest whilst offering that smug smirk.

I narrowed my eyes as I drew on my cigarette. "You want me to believe that you're Carol's boy?"

"Yep, 'fraid so. She was a drug addict, which led to me ending up in care before my parents adopted me in '77."

As I glanced along the landing, I spotted a black woman approaching from the other direction accompanied by a lad who I presumed to be her son. The woman, her waist-length, braided hair swished around her shoulder, appeared to hold something to her ear. I watched as she jabbered away to herself whilst clamping what seemed to be a policeman's styled notebook against her temple. As she slotted her key in the door of flat 120, that answered my next question – Carol Hall no longer lived next door.

Within the space of half an hour, it appeared Tattoo-Girl had taken my flat, and Don and Carol, my neighbours, had also moved out. Although that had clearly happened, I ventured to suggest to my brain that it simply wasn't possible – unless – no.

"No," I shook my head, verbalising my unacceptance that my suited stalker might be telling the truth.

Chris extracted from his jacket pocket what, at first inspection, appeared to be a slim notebook similar to what that black woman had slapped to her ear. On closer inspection, as he rolled it around in his hand, it appeared to be a lump of black plastic. He held it out to me. "Here, take it. Well, look at it, because you can't have it. That's what that woman had held to her ear."

I clamped my cigarette between my lips and tentatively held out my hand.

"Go on. It won't bite," he chuckled.

"What is it?" I quizzed, inspecting what appeared to be made of glass and heavier than I'd expected.

"Press one of the side buttons."

I glanced up at him before searching for a button, raising my eyebrows when the date flashed up on the front. Apart from the odd thing looking like a fancy electronic pocket calculator, it confirmed the time and that today was the 12th of August. "Oh, it's a watch. Bit of a hefty old lump, ain't it? Where's the strap?"

Chris removed it from my grip. "It's a mobile … mobile telephone, digital camera, and a computer. It's got a torch, calculator … all sorts, really. Also, it plays music, plus you can listen to the radio, as well as a pretty nifty GPS navigation system. This one's an iPhone 6S plus, with a 12-megapixel camera, 4K video capability and 64 gig."

Although most of what he just uttered made absolutely bugger-all sense, as I removed my cigarette from my lip, my eye was again drawn to Dublin House opposite. I stepped past him and leaned on the railing. "What are those?" I indicated with my outstretched arm, bemused as to why the tower block opposite seemed to be splatted with what appeared to be parabolic bowls as if the building's façade had succumbed to some freakish disease.

Chris swivelled around, knitted his eyebrows as he followed my gaze and peered into the distance. I glanced back at him, awaiting his answer.

"What? Sorry, what are you pointing at?"

"On the flats. They're everywhere. The building is covered in them."

"Dishes? You're referring to the satellite dishes?"

"Satellite? What, like Viking Two?"

"I have no idea what that is. But, yes, they're TV satellite dishes.

"TV … what, TV from outer space?" I scoffed.

"Oh, hell. This is going to be a lot harder than I thought."

"What is? And please don't mention time travel again. I'll accept there are some bloody strange things afoot, but if you mention Doctor Who again, I'll just walk into town." I glanced at my watch. "Shit, I need to get going," I mumbled, realising that even if I put a bit of a lick on, I'd probably miss my meeting with the twentieth-century's version of Fagin.

"Where are you going in town?" Chris asked, trotting behind me as I powered down the landing.

"The bank," I threw over my shoulder.

"Which bank?"

I halted and swivelled around. "What's it to you unless you're offering a lift?"

"Which bank?" he repeated.

"Midland Bank ... the one at the top of the High Street."

Chris frowned before raising a finger. "Ah, yes. Starbucks. Come on, I've got an idea."

7

Some Mothers Do 'Ave 'Em

"Hi, Chris. Don't tell me … you've run out of clean undies and you've forgotten how to use the washing machine?" the woman's voice jauntily enquired, which emanated from somewhere I couldn't quite pinpoint.

"No," chuckled Chris. "I'm quite domesticated, you know."

"Oh, okay. Well, if that crisis is averted, I won't worry too much. Look, sorry I haven't got long. The bloody school's just rung. They're on their way back because half the kids have all chundered on the coach. Apparently, Oli managed to splatter Miss Havers with his projectile vomits from at least four rows back," she chuckled. "Anyway, summer camp has been cancelled, which is bloody frustrating because Phil and I were going up to the Lakes for that spa weekend. Poor Oli, you know he's got a delicate constitution and always had a penchant for puking since he was a baby. I mean, shut the front door, but he gets green around the gills on an escalator, so projectile vomiting on a stinking coach full of school kids is hardly a surprise—"

"Beth—" Chris threw in, trying to halt the woman's verbal diarrhoea.

"He's always suffered from motion sickness. You remember that time at Disneyland Paris when he covered that kid in puke after coming off the Indiana Jones ride? That was Phil's fault. He should never have snuck Oli on that ride." She briefly came up for air before continuing. "That Charlotte woman, you know, the school secretary who always coos over Phil, bloody annoys me that does, and he just laughs it off. Anyway, she reckons that Norovirus is sweeping the camp like a Californian wildfire, and the tents resemble a scene from *The Exorcist*," she chuckled again.

"Beth—"

"They said the coach will be back at the school by eleven, and can we all get back and be there to pick the kids up? I said that summer camp was a crap idea for Oli. You know how wimpy he can be … Chris, you still there?"

"Beth, for Christ—"

"I think we've spoilt him, you know. He'd probably have turned out differently if we'd had another. Not that Phil and I don't practice enough … Woah!" she boomed. "Sorry, way too much detail to tell my brother," she guffawed before launching into her next volley of pointless conversation. "I know he's my son, but I do wish he wasn't so introverted. God knows where he gets that from because you could hardly accuse Phil or me of being a shrinking violet, could you? Anyway, I don't think Oli actually wanted to go, but Phil said it would do him good to be away from us for a while. Make a man of him, he said. I mean, what bollocks, he's only ten—"

"Beth, can I get a word in edgeways—"

"Sorry, what were you saying? I don't think it's that Norovirus because that's a winter vomiting bug. It's more likely to be some dodgy chicken they didn't cook properly on the campfire. I'm half a mind to get Phil to sue the arse off the bloody school—"

"Beth! Take a breath. I have something to tell you."

"Oh, sorry. Are you alright? You've not had an accident, have you? Christ, is Megan okay?"

"She's fine. I spoke to her this morning. The trip has gone well, and she'll be flying back at the weekend, but—"

"Oh, okay. Are you picking her up? Presumably, she's coming into Heathrow. I'd invite you both around for dinner, but with Oli as he is—"

"Beth!"

"What?"

"I found him."

"Found who?"

"Jason Apsley … y'know, *other* Jason. You remember what Dad said to me?"

"Chris, you're breaking up. I'm driving through the Chalk Hills; you know how shit the reception is through here. What did you say? I thought for a moment there you said Jason Apsley."

"I *did* say Jason Apsley," Chris glanced at his telephone positioned in its cradle in the centre console before waving to the driver of a battered Land Rover, indicating for him to pull out of a parking space at the bottom end of the High Street. "Beth?" he quizzed as he performed a near-perfect parallel parking manoeuvre.

"Chris, what d'you mean?"

I detected a significant shift in the woman's tone. No longer jovial, despite her son, Oliver, pebble dashing some woman called Miss Havers, to a more sombre lilt at the mention of my name. Who she was and how the hell she knew of me, well, that just added to the exponentially growing heap of ridiculousness. Also, I wondered why Chris referred to me as 'other' Jason.

"He's sitting beside me. Gotta say, the poor fella looks a little shell-shocked. But it's definitely him. It's the bloke that Dad said about."

"Other Jason?" Beth barked, who seemed to have lost her chattiness since the mention of my name.

"Yes!"

Apart from the obvious issue that my suited stalker appeared to be holding a telephone conversation in a car – the likes of which I'd only seen in films and, even then, the phone was attached to a cord – the short drive into town gave rise to suggest that altercation with the edge of that concrete step had caused severe brain damage. Not only did the Broxworth Estate appear to have morphed its appearance, but so did the rest of Fairfield.

The wireless programme Chris had his radio tuned into featured the Olympics and the men's cycling team's gold medal they achieved yesterday. The commentator suggested that even at this early stage, Team GB was on course to supersede the twenty-nine golds achieved at the London Olympics in 2012.

This was a problem.

Firstly, the Olympics finished last week. An event held in Montreal, not Rio. Also, I recall the gold medal haul was significantly lower than twenty-odd. I knew this to be a fact because I remember David Wilkie being interviewed by David Colman after winning one of only three golds that the British team managed to achieve.

Also, my now missing Cortina, although not new, as in just off the production line, was an XL model with all the latest refinements, like a cigarette lighter; two-speed wipers; leather gear knob, not to mention the built-in radio. However, this thing, which Chris had stated was a BMW X5, was akin to something out of Captain Scarlet and the Mysterons. I suspected it put the Spectrum Patrol Car to shame and probably sported an ejector seat like Bond's Aston Martin DB5.

Apart from giving the appearance I was sitting in the cockpit of some supersonic fighter jet, Chris's motor made my Cortina appear – well – basic.

"Oh, Chris, you're not still on that wild goose chase about what you reckon Dad said?" the Beth woman exclaimed with more than a hint of frustration.

"He's here beside me." Chris nodded at his lump of plastic that he reckoned was a phone, amongst a million other things, most of which I had no idea about. That said, I couldn't fathom how it could be a torch since no space for batteries existed. Chris nodded at me and then at that lump of plastic. "Jason, say hello to my little sister."

I side-eyed him.

"Go on," he encouraged, whilst removing his seat belt. Something he'd insisted I reciprocate when leaving the

Broxworth, stating it's the law to wear one when I'd said I didn't normally bother.

"Hello," I announced, feeling somewhat daft, as if talking to myself.

"Who's that you've got in the car with you? Chris ... Chris, is this some bloody joke?"

"Beth ... look, I know how this sounds. And believe you me, although I made that promise to Dad, I, like you, thought it was just the poor old boy losing his mind. But listen, I have found *other* Jason."

"Chris, what on earth are you on about? You're not making any sense."

"Can you drop Oliver off at the neighbours for an hour or so? Then, meet me in Starbucks in town, and I'll show you."

"No, not really ... I'm not palming Oli off on Donna to then traipse into town on some stupid pretence that you've unearthed a time traveller. Bloody hell, Chris, should you be driving? It sounds like you've had a ruddy skinful. Have you been eating properly while Megan's away? You are looking after yourself, aren't you?"

"Beth, I can look after myself. I have a drawer full of clean underwear and can wield a tin opener with the best of them. Look, Oli will be okay at—"

"Up yours too, knob-head!" Beth boomed.

I glanced at Chris, who winced at his phone. Although I was an only child and missed out on the joy of a sibling relationship, this Beth woman's tone could only be described as odd.

"Beth, you okay?"

"Sorry, Chris. Some see-you-next-Tuesday driving a puke-coloured Lada just hooted and gave me the finger. Now the tosser's up my arse. Fuck you too, dickhead!" Beth bellowed again.

"Beth?"

"Sorry, I was shouting at the tit behind me, not you. What were you saying?"

"Beth, I've found the man who Dad reckons he took the place of in 1976. Jason Apsley is here with us right now, and he's the spit of those pictures of Dad. You won't believe this, but he's even got a yellow Cortina."

"Did have," I muttered, musing that this Beth woman was somewhat foul-mouthed, suspecting I wouldn't warm to the cut of her jib. Also, she'd mentioned that the other driver, who she seemed intent on shouting at, was driving a Lada. Now, I'm no car fanatic, but I'm pretty sure that a Lada is a Russian car manufacturer, and no such heaps of crap had made it to this side of the Iron Curtain.

"Oh, bloody hell, you haven't been rummaging through Jordan's bedroom and found your son's stash of his wacky baccy? Is that it? While Megan's away, you've spent all week smoking his secret stash of weed, and now you're imagining time travellers?"

There it was again – time travel. My suited stalker had mentioned it, and now his foul-mouthed sister also appeared to be of a mind to mention the ridiculous. Although, on a positive note, this Beth woman seemed to agree with me on this one – time travel – ridiculous. However, the newspaper and radio reports were worrying.

"Beth, please. Meet me in Starbucks."

Beth huffed. "Christ, this better be good and not one of your practical jokes. I'll call Donna and see if she can pick Oli up. Which Starbucks are you going to?"

"Great. Top of the High Street. Y'know, the one that used to be the Midland Bank."

I side-eyed Chris again. That was the second time he'd suggested that the bank was no longer where it should be. Apart from the surreal events taking place, if the bank had suddenly morphed into this thing called Starbucks and my safety deposit box had miraculously vanished, I feared this morning's events thus far would pale into insignificance.

I'd secured over sixty grands worth of diamonds, which should be tucked away in that bank's vault. If that was no longer the case, that meeting with a couple of dodgy gentlemen I should be attending in less than twenty minutes could prove to be somewhat tricky. I'm led to believe the one whose name I didn't know was not the sort who took too kindly to being let down.

Despite my concerns regarding the consequences of a failed cash and diamond exchange, as I glanced out of the side window, I spotted what appeared to be more shop rebranding. It seemed that Fairfield's Chamber of Commerce had pulled an all-nighter when embarking on giving the whole town a facelift. Like the Wavy Line Store on the estate, Chelsea Girl also appeared to have gone through a rebranding, now calling itself River Island.

I feared for Midland Bank.

If my bank had changed its name but still maintained its vault, all would be okay. However, if this thing called Starbucks was now in its place, that would leave me wishing I had died on those concrete steps.

"Alright, alright. I'll give Donna a bell and see you there in, say … about fifteen?"

"Great. Be prepared for a shock, though," Chris chuckled, whilst prodding the screen and tapping a couple of buttons on the car's inbuilt TV screen before turning to me. "Okay, you ready?"

"What's Star thingy?" I quizzed, detecting a tremor in my voice.

"Starbucks? Oh, it's … you remember the Wimpy?"

"Yeah … don't tell me they've changed their name overnight, too?"

"Kind of. Look, Starbucks is where you buy coffee and drinks, like you could in the Wimpy."

"And that has taken over Midland Bank."

"Yeah … I dunno. Must have been at least ten years ago. I can't really remember."

"Where's the bank now, then?"

"I'm pretty sure it got taken over by HSBC."

"I don't get this. How come my bank has disappeared overnight?"

"Jason. Look around you." Chris animatedly waved his hands, indicating the High Street. "Nothing has changed overnight. I get that believing you've time travelled is a bit of a head spinner. Christ, don't you think I'm a bit bemused by it too? But look around you. As much as I was convinced locating you was not going to happen, here you are."

"Jesus, I've had enough of this." I threw open the car door and galloped my way up the High Street, so hell-bent on reaching the bank I didn't even bother to close the passenger door.

"Jason, hang on!"

Despite the hollering of my new stalker, I trotted along, trying to ignore the clear evidence that Woolworths and Bejam's freezer centre also appeared to have morphed into different stores. Also, as I hightailed up the significantly wider pavement than I recall traversing last week, I spotted that, in their infinite wisdom, the council had removed the bank of red phone boxes, and shoppers needed to weave in and out the chicane system of the randomly placed raised flower beds.

Clearly, either one of three things had occurred. Firstly, the town had undergone the mother-of-all mammoth makeovers in the space of one night. Or secondly, I was still lying concussed in that stairwell, and I was now experiencing a rather vivid dream. Or thirdly – no. No, that was stupid. However, as I reached my bank that was now, as Chris suggested, called Starbucks, that third option jostled for position as the most likely reason the world appeared to have changed – time travel.

"Bollocks," I muttered.

Ignoring the Starbucks's illuminated lettering, the large picture windows and the young couple sipping coffee at a table near the window, the Edwardian stone building appeared not to have changed. In fact, the stone façade still stated Midland Bank, despite the golden griffin sign switching into a green and white crowned mermaid.

"E equals MC squared," I muttered, whilst stroking my thumb and forefinger across my goatee beard. One of the debating societies I'd dabbled in before the conversations became too ridiculous, when at university in the '50s, centred around Einstein's theories along with the calculations of the Dutch Mathematician Willem Van something or other, his name escaping me at this precise moment. And then, a couple of years ago, I'd read a paper by Frank Tipler and his cylinder theory about the possibilities of time travel.

However, as I mused about the theories of a collection of eminent scientists, I doubted that I, after cracking the back of my head, had managed to time travel like the nameless character in one of Mr Wells's books. Conversely, despite those doubts, there was irrefutable evidence that something rather peculiar was afoot.

Two lads, I guess in their early twenties, hovered by the entrance to what was my bank. Despite Chris's and Tattoo-Girl's insistence that today was the 12th of August 2016, I thought I'd seek a third opinion. I stepped forward. "Excuse me?"

"Yo, bro," the taller of the two jutted his chin at me as I offered a welcoming smile.

"I'm sorry?"

The shorter chap, wearing what appeared to be a jacket made from a sleeping bag, similar to the sort of thing I'd used back in my days of orienteering across the North Yorkshire Moors with the Boys' Brigade, and apart from the fact he must have been sweating profusely, appeared nervous by my presence. He nudged his mate and nodded, presumably suggesting they should move on.

"Stop your baiting, bro," Taller muttered, his eyes scanning the street whilst sniffing repeatedly.

"Bounce, bro," suggested Shorty to Taller whilst offering me a sucking teeth expression.

Bemused by their oddish vocabulary and unwelcome greetings, I bashed on. "Could you tell me what today is, please?"

"It ain't your day, bro," Taller muttered, before jutting his head again. "Yo dizzy, bro?"

"Dizzy?"

"Nutter. You got us wrong, bro. Ya feds nut goin' to pull no food from us heads," he announced, pulling the inside of his jacket pockets out, showing they were devoid of any food.

"Food?" I quizzed, now completely losing the thread of this conversation. "I'm not asking for food, just what today's date is, that's all."

They exchanged a glance before Shorty took up the conversation. "He's no Fed, bro, nut looking like dat," he smirked. "Yo, dizzy man, bounce, bro."

"Sorry, looking like what?" I glanced down at my attire, thinking their comment was a bit rich, considering how they were dressed. Both lads were clearly in the need of a sturdy leather belt to hold up their jeans, which appeared to have sagged below the waistline.

"Oi!" shouted an elderly woman, whose diminutive stature made Shorty appear positively leggy, as she repeatedly jabbed the end of her walking stick into my chest. "None of your drug dealing here, you good-for-nothing layabouts. Go on, off with you!" she barked, leaving me with a gaping mouth whilst the two lads, whom I had no idea what they'd said, slithered away into a side alley.

"And you," she jabbed her stick again. "Should be ashamed of yourself. A man your age dealing drugs … I don't know what the world's coming to. It's the bloody government's fault … sodding Tories. Useless, all of them. My Craig is about your age, and he's respectable. He's a police officer, y'know," she offered a pronounced nod as if confirming she'd played the trump card. Then, after one more forceful poke to nail home her views, she loudly tutted her disapproval and stepped back into the throng of shoppers traversing the High Street.

"Oh, excuse me," I called out to her.

"Don't give me any of your lip, son. I might be an oldie, but I ain't afraid to give you a damn good clip around the ear."

"How old is your Craig? What year is this?"

"Turned forty this year, he did."

"And what year was he born?"

"What's this got to do with your lazy, layabout attitude?"

"Year?"

"Thick sort, are you?"

I raised my eyebrows.

"I said my Craig was forty. So that's '76, yer daft 'apeth. That ruddy hot summer which I reckon you're too young to remember," she barked before offering that pronounced tut.

"Jason, Christ man, hold up," panted Chris as he bounded towards me.

"This nitwit with you?" she jabbed her stick at Chris, performing a similar chest-poking routine on him as she had me. "I suggest you get this Frank-Spencer idiot off the streets.

He's liable to get himself in all sorts of bother, especially dressed like that. I dunno, some mothers do 'ave 'em."

Chris gently palmed away her stick, offering a tight smile. "Leave it with me."

"Mind you do. He's that drugged up the poor sod don't know if he's coming or going, let alone what bloody year it is."

Chris nodded as she turned on me, waving that stick again. "It's 2016, you silly sod. And if you carry on pumping that crap into your arm, you won't see 2017, I can tell you. My Craig sees your sort all the time. Get a proper job, you lazy waster."

8

The Music of the Night

The coffee was good. The fact that my safety deposit box was apparently stuck four decades in the past was not so. That said, apart from now being penniless, I wouldn't have to face the man with no name at a meeting I was purportedly forty years late for.

Whilst we occupied a table, positioned roughly where I thought the bank teller should be perched, Chris excitedly rabbitted on about his father. With the aid of a plethora of hand gestures, he drivelled on about the man who he reckoned had the same name and was a doppelgänger for my good self. Also, claiming he'd time-travelled from 2019 to 1976 and apparently taken my place. Hmmm.

After a few minutes of listening to his excitable ramblings, I glazed over. Whilst allowing his chatter to mingle with the background noise, I took a moment to try and rationalise this absurdity.

The three possibilities I'd contemplated when charging up the High Street to explain this morning's events simply didn't cut the mustard. Time travel, according to most scientists, was technically possible if you could somehow travel faster than the speed of light. Now, when leaving my flat about an hour ago, I'd put a bit of a lick-on as I'd zipped along the landing. However, nothing close to a couple of hundred-thousand miles per second. Also, mathematically, travelling backwards through time, as this excitable idiot who continued animatedly waving his arms around reckoned his father had achieved, was simply not scientifically feasible.

The possibility that I was dreaming whilst still lying in that stairwell also didn't hold water because my t-shirt sported the dirty mark left by the end of that curmudgeonly woman's walking stick when she'd repeatedly thrust it at my chest. As for the whole of Fairfield undergoing a makeover, well, that was as ridiculous as the rest of my thoughts when trying to explain my somewhat bewildering situation.

"So, what d'you reckon? Jason, did you hear me?"

When hearing my name, I glanced up at Chris, who appeared to have given his jaw muscles a break, now sporting a raised eyebrow expression.

"Sorry, what?"

"The Cortina. Let's check to see if it's yours."

"What?"

"I was saying about Dad's Cortina … oh, here she is. Beth," he called out to a flustered-looking thirty-something woman who scraped her blonde hair away from her face as she barrelled towards us. Dressed in the tightest pair of jeans I've ever seen, I pondered if she'd been stitched into them. Unlike her brother, I guessed she'd benefited from an athletic gene pool from her parents.

Chris hopped up from his chair, leaving me to stare back at my coffee. Despite his obvious excitement, I harboured no desire to chat to his sister about her son's puking or the aggressive nature of other drivers careering around town in Russian cars.

"Christ, it's easier to locate a steaming heap of rocking-horse shit than a free parking space in this ruddy town. You won't believe it, but I had to park all the way over near the top of Timber Hill. Even then, some bell-end reckoned he'd been waiting for the space when I snuck in," she announced, plonking herself onto the free seat beside me.

"I got you a Mocha. Is Oli okay?"

"Oh, thanks. Yeah, he'll be fine. Donna is picking him up. Like father, like son. You know Phil chunders at the drop of a hat. That time he threw up at Mum and Dad's anniversary made the cherry-puke scene from *The Witches of Eastwick* seem tame," she chortled. "Sometimes I'm half tempted to batter my husband with a poker myself, God love him."

"Oh, right. So, as I said, you ain't going to believe this! Can I present—"

"You know, talking of battering to death, the roads are full of wankers these days. No one's got any bloody patience. After that knob in that Lada hooted me, I told that turd who fought me for that parking space that he should learn some frigging manners. That's before I told him to swivel and to go fuck himself—"

"Beth." Chris held his hands out, indicating to where I perched, staring down at my coffee. "Ta-dah!" he announced in a sing-song voice.

Keeping my head low, I sipped my coffee whilst wondering what string of expletives were about to pour out of this woman's mouth next.

"Ta-bloody-dah what?"

"Jason Apsley, AKA *other* Jason, meet my little sister, Beth."

"Bollocks it is," Beth retorted before offering a short, mirthless laugh.

Although not wishing to engage in conversation, I glanced up and offered an over-exaggerated, tight smile. Chris kept his hands aloft as if showing off some wondrous creation he'd just produced. I half expected him to announce, 'here's one I made earlier' in true Blue Peter style.

"Fuck me," she slowly announced, her bottom lip remaining slack as she halted the advance of her coffee cup towards her gaping mouth.

Chris slapped that photo on the table and jabbed a finger at it. "Look, see what I mean? He's the spit of Dad. Well, Dad from those old photos."

Keeping her coffee cup poised mid-air, Beth swivelled her eyes down at the photo and then back at me, repeating this oscillating manoeuvre every few seconds.

"And, get this." Chris jabbed his index finger at me whilst nudging his sister's arm with his elbow. "He actually thinks it's 1976! He's convinced of it, would you believe? Mad, ain't it?"

"Bollocks, as Dad would say," she muttered. "My God, he frigging looks just like him." Beth placed her cup down before pointing at my ears. "Look, they're as big and flappy as Dad's were," she guffawed.

"I know! Look, look at his clothes," Chris enthusiastically gestured at me with a wagging finger. "The flares ... the collar on that jacket. He's like something out of Starsky and Hutch. I'm half expecting Huggy Bear to rock up," he chuckled.

"Who's Starsky and Hutch?" I quizzed.

"Sorry?" they both blurted in unison.

I shrugged.

"Fecking amazeballs!" she announced, as she ran her eyes up and down my attire. "I could have sworn the original series was on TV before I was born."

"Late seventies, I think," Chris chimed in.

"Fuckerdedoda. Fucking amazeballs," she muttered, peering at me like I was some grotesque specimen in a Petri dish.

I narrowed my eyes at her statement, presuming they were two more words plucked from her repertoire of peculiar expletives. Now, look, I'm a man of the world, but apart from the residence of that damn estate, I'd not encountered many women who trotted out obscenities at such a rate.

"Hey, Jason. I've just thought. Was Carol pregnant when you lived on the estate?"

I nodded and huffed before grabbing my coffee. Despite the concerns about my situation, I was becoming a wee bit miffed that my new stalker and his potty-mouthed sister appeared to be enjoying poking fun at me like a couple of school bullies picking on the weird kid in the playground. Also, Chris had said, 'when you lived on the estate' – *when* being the operative word. As far as I was concerned, I'd spoken to Carol last night. And yes, after trotting out a string of obscenities about the hot weather and how being pregnant didn't help, she'd clipped her son around the ear for whinging.

A small, shy boy, who this chap reckoned he was the grown-up version of.

"Wow! Whoo-hoo," Chris announced as he flung his head back before rocking forward on his chair and waving his hands at Beth as he'd earlier gestured at me. "So, here she is … Beth was that unborn baby. As far as you're concerned, yesterday, she was still a few months from being born. Now she's my thirty-nine-year-old amazing little sister."

"Really, is that so?" I sarcastically spat back.

"Frig! He sounds just like Dad!"

Whilst sporting a deadpan face, I slowly shook my head at her. Unfortunately, it appeared she was also bought into this ridiculous notion that this other Apsley bloke and I were the same man.

"Say something else."

"Like what?" I shrugged.

"I don't know. Anything. I just need to hear your voice. You can recite the Lord's Prayer, Dickens, or the entire script from the Phantom of the Opera for all I care. Just say something, man."

I raised an eyebrow. Despite that brief foray into Sunday School, I'd never been one for religion, so the Lord's Prayer was out. Dickens, well, yes, I'd read a few at school but couldn't remember any particular lines. As for Phantom of the Opera, I had no idea what that was. However, considering my surreal situation, H.G. Wells seemed appropriate. Although this was not sorting out the issue of my missing safety deposit box, I thought I'd comply to get the charade over with. Anyway, this Beth woman didn't appear to be prepared to relent from her request anytime soon. I cleared my throat, thinking of a line.

"There are four dimensions, three which we call the three planes of space, and the fourth, time."

"The Time Machine," Chris confirmed.

I nodded. "With what you're suggesting, it seemed rather apt."

Still gawping at me as if I'd grown a second head, Beth breathed in and exhaled as if trying to calm her breathing. "An odd twang, but that's Dad's voice."

"South Africa. I've been there for years. I reckon I picked up some of the accent."

"See! I told you." Chris excitedly wagged his finger at me whilst addressing his sister. "That's what Dad said to me. He reckoned the bloke he replaced had just returned from South Africa. We always thought Dad had lived there. But when he spouted that gibberish at me, he reckoned he'd never been there."

Beth shook her head. "Chris, is this a setup? I wasn't there when Dad died. Have you set this whole thing up?"

"Beth."

I detected the sharpness in his retort.

"Chris, I'm sorry. I know you wouldn't do that. But, frig me, how the effin' hell can he be this *other* Jason?"

"I don't know. As I said, I didn't believe it would happen. I just felt compelled to do as Dad asked."

"Chris," she hissed. "Time travel isn't possible."

"Agreed!" I stabbed into their conversation.

"Hey Jason, tell Beth how much you paid for a packet of cigarettes yesterday." He nudged his head forward and grinned. "Go on."

I huffed and shook my head.

"Come on, play the game."

"About five shillings." I dismissively waved my hand as I converted the sum in my head. "About twenty-five pence, I think."

Chris and Beth nodded at each other and giggled before Beth threw in the next question.

"What did you watch on TV last night?"

"As it happens, I don't watch much television."

"Oh." She seemed a little disappointed. "Oh, I know," she exclaimed, her excitement returning, now almost hopping up and down on her chair. "So, go on, who do you think is the Prime Minister and the President of the USA? I feel like Emmett Brown," she chuckled whilst nodding at Chris, who grinned back with a glint in his eye.

"Why have I got to say this?"

Beth patronisingly patted my hand, an action I suspected she would perform on Puking-Oliver when her son wasn't in the mood to play games. "Come on, play along."

"I caught the end of *Tomorrow's World* before nipping over to the bar in the community centre … which isn't there now." The last four words were more of a question in my head as I tried to compute how that could be. "And, as you seem insistent, Big Jim Callaghan and Jimmy Carter. There, you satisfied? Now, can we discuss where my—"

"Tomorrow's World!" she exclaimed, interrupting me. "OMG, amazeballs! Chris, he said Tomorrow's World!" she guffawed again. "What were they saying about the future? Was it all flying cars and robots doing the housework?"

"Is this relevant to my situation?"

Beth expectantly raised her eyebrows at me. "Just answer our questions, man. You're just like my husband Phil. I can never get a straight answer out of the bloke unless I'm suggesting an early night. That instantly gets a positive response." Her chuckle quickly morphing into an embarrassed whine. "Oh, sorry, way too much detail." She dismissively waved her hand in the air as if to bat away her statement regarding her husband's positive responses to a tumble in the sheets. "Come on, spit it out."

Apart from her obvious good looks, I thought her husband was a saint for putting up with the woman. "Bloody hell. I was only half watching it. That Judith Hann woman was at some factory where some bloke had invented a machine that would re-use rubbish by sorting paper from plastic and general bric-à-brac. As are most things on that programme, I suspect unlikely to become a commercially viable prospect. I think they called it recycling, meaning re-using something."

"Bric-à-brac! My God, that's the sort of word Mum or Jess would have trotted out," she again loudly chortled.

"Beth," Chris paused to nod in my direction. "Jess," he hissed.

The name Jess caused me to prick up my ears. A common girl's name, for sure, and probably short for Jessica. Back in the '50s, my girlfriend gave birth to our daughter. The relationship broke down. I moved away, and we never kept in touch. Assuming I hadn't time travelled, my daughter, Jessica, would be twenty by now.

"Oh, hell," muttered Beth, her jocular persona melting away. She picked up her coffee and turned away from me.

"Who's Jess? Can I ask?"

I detected concern briefly skate across their faces before Chris repeatedly glanced between me and Beth. "Err ... well, we think—"

"No! Hang on, Chris," Beth interrupted, slamming her cup down before pointing at me. "As ridiculous as all this is, this might just prove who he is. So, come on, Mr Jason Apsley, do you know a Jess?"

"My daughter ... Jessica Redmond. I haven't seen her since she was a baby, so she took her mother's surname."

"Wow, what a clusterfuck fucktangle," she mumbled, gawping at me with an expression of mesmerised wonder.

9

Bad Manners

Whilst the indecipherable loud chatter continued, which emanated from all tables that flanked ours, the three of us just shot looks at each other after Beth had trotted out two more somewhat odd expletives. The 'fuck' bit I understood. The remainder of her verbalisation of surprise was a complete mystery.

"So, do you know Jessica Redmond, then?" I asked, keen to know if she was the same person as my daughter but also to break the gawping spell Beth appeared to have fallen into.

Beth side-eyed Chris, whose shrug appeared to be a non-verbal approval for her to answer my question.

"She's our half-sister. Dad's daughter … your daughter, if you see what I mean."

"Right. Course she is. This Jess was born on the 17th of June '56, by any chance?"

"She was. That's Jess's birthday," Chris sombrely affirmed.

"Hell, d'you think this is actually him?" Although she continued to stare at me, I assumed she was talking to her brother. "I mean, the look, the voice, the fact he actually thinks it's 1976. Him knowing Jess, let alone the Noel Edmond's look and the David Soul get-up with the retro clothes."

"It's got to be him."

"Jesus, this is mega nuts."

"Beth … Beth. Listen to this," Chris shifted forward in his seat. "He thinks he lives in that flat. You know, the one that Carol lived next door to. The one you and I lived in before … well, you know. He actually had a slanging match with some woman who lives there."

Beth turned from where she'd been studying me like some exotic caged animal and waved her finger at Chris. "He actually thought he still lived there?"

"Yeah," he chuckled. "He had the right old Harry about it."

"What did he say to her, this woman?"

"I chased him up the stairwell … well, that's after he chased this woman, but—"

"Why was he chasing her?"

"No, he wasn't. Look, it's getting a bit confusing. He reckoned he got mugged, so he had to nip back to *his* flat to grab some spare change."

"Mugged? Mugged by who? Did he say?"

"Err … excuse me, I am here, you know," I interjected.

"Just be quiet for a moment. Drink your coffee and behave."

I opened my mouth to protest, but no words formed as she patronisingly patted my hand and offered a whimsical smile before readdressing Chris. "Start from the beginning. What did he actually say when you met him?" Beth grabbed her cup and swigged a mouthful of coffee. Mocha, as Chris called it, whatever that was, whilst her brother launched into a rather enthusiastic recounting of this morning's events.

As he machine-gunned out the story, interrupted by a few 'no ways', the liberally interjected 'fuck me' and a couple of 'amazeballs' from Beth, I grabbed a saucer from the next table to use as an ashtray and lit up a cigarette.

I hadn't noticed it earlier, but the cigarette appeared longer than usual, slightly surprised the packet didn't state King Size. As I plucked up the pack and studied the branding, Chris and Beth continued their overly enthusiastic conversation. However, as I dragged on my cigarette, I detected the general hubbub around me quieten to almost library status. When I glanced around to assess the reason for the instant hush that had descended, it appeared the vast majority in the packed café were all staring at me.

As I flicked the ash on the saucer, I wondered if this was why. I shrugged, thinking if the waitresses had forgotten to put out the ashtrays when setting up, a saucer would suffice – no big deal.

"Sir," aggressively bellowed the chap who earlier served us our drinks from some swanky Italian-styled coffee machine.

"Me?" I poked my chest.

"Yes, you! What the hell are you doing?"

"Oh, sorry. No ashtrays, mate."

"Frigging hell!" boomed Beth, before snatching my cigarette from my mouth and lobbing it into my half-drunk coffee. She swivelled in her chair and bellowed at everyone who continued to gawp in my direction. "Sorry! Sorry, everyone. He's ... well, he's not been around for a while ... he didn't know."

Beth's explanation that I didn't know something halted the chatter from the odd table that hadn't already stopped to stare, resulting in about forty sets of eyes boring down upon us. Some shook their heads, others tutted – all glowered at me, showing their disdain.

"Where's he been? The fucking moon?" boomed a voice from behind a pillar.

"No, he's just been ... away," Beth shouted.

The owner of that voice popped his head around the pillar. Everyone, including the three behind the counter, held their breath as the verbal exchange between Beth and this chap kicked off.

"Ex-con, is he?" the large chap called out as he stood. Going by the extensive covering of tattoos up both arms, I presumed he must have been friends with the girl who'd taken my flat.

"Sorry?" barked Beth, seemingly unperturbed by the man's size and blatant aggression.

"Your mate, there." He thumbed in my direction. "Just got out, has he? Looks like a lifer. I shared a cell with a few over the years, and that twat looks just like one."

"I've got a baby, you prick," announced the woman sitting at the same table as she gently winded the child nestled onto her chest.

The large, tattooed chap stepped forward and pointed at Beth. "Suggest you take the twat home before someone sorts him out. My boy ain't 'ere to breathe in this prick's cigarette smoke."

Now, popping to one side that the issue appeared to be the fact that I'd lit a cigarette, I'd been in enough tricky situations in my time to know this was about to kick off. Although this Beth woman was starting to royally piss me off, I knew I'd have to do the gentlemanly thing and ensure this thug didn't overstep the mark.

However, Beth slapped her hand on my chest before I could spring into action, thus forcing me back into my chair before addressing the bloke who looked like a skinhead who'd misplaced his eight-hole Doc Martens.

"Sod off, you knob-end. I've said we're sorry. He didn't know you can't smoke in here. Now, go fuck yourself."

A murmur of 'Ooos' rolled around the café as the skinhead appeared to ponder Beth's suggestion.

"Oi, shut your gob, bitch. You should be at home wiv your pinny on, looking after your 'usband, not …" he grinned and paused his rant as Beth hopped up from her chair. "Jesus … Beff Baker, ain't it?" he chuckled.

"Babe?" called out the woman, now bouncing the baby enough to cause the poor sod's head to wobble.

The skinhead turned to the woman. "Hey, it's Beff. You know my brief's missus. Phil Baker's other 'alf."

"Buster," Beth announced.

"Yeah, that's me, girl. They call me Bloodvessel after that singing geezer bloke."

"Yeah, Phil said as much. You're far more handsome, though."

"Oh, cheers, Beff. How's your old man?"

"He's good; all the better for not having to represent you for a while. I take it you've stopped dishing out GBH or just not been caught bending people in half?" she chuckled. "Phil always said you were good fun to represent."

"Yeah, well, gotta go straight, ain't I. As you can see, got a nipper now, ain't I. Cheryl's got me on the straight and narrow, ain't that right, girl?"

As the woman bouncing the baby nodded, the chatter in the café restarted, as if in a flick of a switch when everyone realised there was nothing to see. As I witnessed the altercation play out, I thought it somewhat odd how the vast majority held aloft a similar-looking device that Chris owned, which he claimed was a camera, torch, and a million other things besides.

"I'm a bouncer up at Luton Airport, now."

"Security Operative."

"Yeah, that's the word," he grinned, nodding at Beth. "Course, I still bounce a few clowns about on the door of the Murderer's Pub on a Saturday night when doing a spot of moonlighting. Keep that to yourself though, 'cos it's unofficial like."

"Mum's the word," Beth tapped her nose. "Anyway, good for you. I know Phil will be pleased for you."

"Say hi to Phil for me."

"Will do."

"Hey, I 'ear your old dad pegged it. Sorry about that."

"Thanks," Beth sighed. "His health left him after Mum passed last year."

"Yeah, sad one, that. Y'know, he was the only teacher that took any interest in me. I remember the day he retired. The whole bleedin' school was packed out to give him a bleedin' good send-off. Mr Apsley was the best teacher the City School ever had. Top bloke, your dad."

"Thanks, Buster. Oh, have you met my brother Chris?"

"How's it hanging, mate?" Buster thrust out his hand.

"To the left, usually," quipped Chris, as he grabbed the hand offered.

"Oh, nice one," he chuckled. "You're just like your old fella. He was always joking about. Y'know, your dad was like that Mystic Meg woman. I still remember how he used to tell stories about the future. Made us laugh, he did. I reckon that's why he was such a good teacher. Y'know, not being a total twat like all the others."

Beth and Chris exchanged a glance. I'd always been pretty good at reading faces, and I knew this thug's comment had resonated with both of them.

"Yeah," Beth hesitated. "Dad loved his little stories, didn't he?"

"Yeah. Y'know, I still remember when he predicted that we'd all be hooked on something he called social media. That was back in the '90s. Wasn't wrong, was he?"

"No, he wasn't," mumbled Chris, shooting a look at Beth.

"My Cheryl's got her 'ead stuck in her phone all day long." He turned to her. "Ain't that right, girl?" She didn't respond, focusing on the screen of her portable telephone thingamajig now the baby on her chest appeared settled. "See," he chuckled, before turning to me. "So, who's this prick, then?"

I leapt to my feet and eyeballed him. Although a big chap, and despite this morning's altercation, a situation I hadn't been prepared for, I could more than handle myself. Anyway, I was having a super-shit day and being called a prick by some skinhead called Buster Blood-Whatever just about topped it off. "Don't call me a prick."

"Prick. You're the prick who finks it's okay to smoke. So yeah, *prick*." He feigned a headbutt to reinforce the word.

"Buster," hissed Beth.

"You look kinda familiar. We done time togever?"

Once again, that library hush descended. As I glanced left, I spotted the synchronised raising of those portable telephones as all other patrons presumably anticipated the resumption of hostilities. Forty-odd sets of eyes flicked back and forth from their telephone screens to Buster and me as we squared up to each other.

Despite Beth and Chris hissing both our names in an attempt at some kind of agitated détente, there appeared to be a strong possibility that this lump and I were about to come to blows. However, the conversation the skinhead and Beth had just exchanged distracted my thoughts.

At the end of this month, after moving into my new house, I was due to start a new career as a teacher up at the Eaton, City of Fairfield, School – colloquially known as the City School. Buster mentioned that he'd been taught by a teacher of the same name. Now, this lump of gristle was, I presumed, in his late thirties to early forties, making him roughly my age.

This posed a few issues. Firstly, the school, back in the late '40s and early '50s, when I attended, was a boys' grammar school. This bouncer bloke just didn't seem the sort to have frequented such a place. Also, I very much doubted he would have managed to pass his eleven-plus exam. And, at no point had there been a teacher with the same name as me – I think I might have remembered that fact.

So, either this situation was due to my hallucinations after cracking my head open, or – or the ridiculous. That other crazy possibility was that Chris and Beth's father had time-travelled, taken my place in 1976, and become a teacher at the school as I had planned. Also, I couldn't ignore the fact that Buster had referred to his schooling days in the '90s. Realistically, that couldn't be the 1890s because that would make him about ninety years old. And if he meant the 1990s, well, as far as I was concerned, that was nearly twenty years in the future.

However, my first priority was to avoid getting my head split open for the second time in as many hours.

"No, fella. I've not done time. Look, I'm sorry about the cigarette. I've been living in South Africa and was unaware you can't smoke in cafés anymore." I held out my hand. "Shake?"

"Beff, who'd you say this twat is?"

"That," Beth pointed at me. "That is Jason Apsley."

10

Groundhog Day

Buster appeared to roll Beth's statement around in his brain. The inordinate amount of time that passed before realisation hit suggested he definitely didn't pass his eleven-plus exam.

"Ah … got the same name as your old dad. He's family, then?"

"Yes … he's a cousin," piped up Chris.

Beth raised an eyebrow at her brother, who shrugged back.

"Okay, I won't rip his head off then," he chuckled, side-eyeing Beth and ignoring my offer of a handshake. "Don't be a twat, Apsley. I suggest you take a leaf out of your uncle's book. Otherwise, I'll need to tap up Beff's old man for his legal skills again. I'm kinda enjoying being out of stir, so don't give me a reason to rip your bollocks off."

Beth grabbed the skinhead's tree-trunk arm. "Buster, we'll sort him out."

With a curl of his lip, he nodded at me, a gesture suggesting if Beth and Chris didn't, he would. After presumably accepting that he didn't need to bend me in half or tear my gonads free, he placed a kiss on Beth's cheek.

"Remind your old man that if he ever needs any help ... you know, sorting out any twats, he only has to shout."

"I will. Now, try not to kill anyone this week," quipped Beth. "Phil's up to his eyeballs at the moment, and the last thing he needs is to try to keep you out of prison."

"Yeah, I'll try. Not easy, though, not with so many dickheads about." He shot me a look as I retook my seat.

"Christ, Beth, who the hell was that?" Chris hissed.

"Buster Bloodvessel."

"I gathered that. I take it he doesn't sing as well?"

"No," Beth chortled. "He acquired the rather apt moniker because of the veins on his head that look like they're about to explode. Also, his size. His real name is Sebastian."

"Well, he doesn't look like a Sebastian. He's one of Phil's clients, I take it?"

"Yeah, used to be one of Phil's best," she chuckled, before her face dropped as she swivelled around and poked a finger at me. "What the hell are we going to do with him?"

"Err ... do you mind? As I said a moment ago, I am here. And you're not going to do anything with me."

"Jason—"

"Sorry, Chris," I interrupted, jabbing my finger at him, then Beth and, akin to a well-trained gunner in a Panzer tank, back to Chris, pausing while considering which ridiculous question I planned to ask next. "Your father, Jason Apsley, looks like me?"

Beth and Chris exchanged a glance before both affirming with a nod. "Identical. Well, to those old photos, not in recent years, of course," added Chris.

"And you say he died a few weeks ago, aged eighty-two? And, like me, was born on the 30th March 1934?"

Chris grimaced before answering. "Hmmm, well, technically, yes. You see, the trouble is when he was rambling on about your existence, Dad reckoned he was born in 1977."

Beth side-eyed Chris and tutted.

I groaned before continuing, firing out my questions like Bamber Gascoigne, although not offering a starter for ten. "He has a daughter called Jess Redmond, who has the same name as my daughter, born on the same day?"

After that quick glance at each other, they nodded.

"And your father was a teacher—"

"Deputy head," interjected Beth. "He was deputy head, not a teacher."

"Okay, the deputy head up at the City School. Which is also the very place I start my new job in a couple of weeks at the beginning of the new term."

"Teaching science and maths, by any chance?" quizzed Chris.

"Yes—"

"Head of department?"

I narrowed my eyes at him as I leaned forward. "Yeah. But—"

"Good God, he is Dad," muttered Beth.

"Hang on. Your father taught at the City School from when? When did he start there?"

"1976 … September 1976," mumbled Beth.

Bemused how this could happen, my next question seemed somewhat pointless based on the soggy cigarette butt that now swam about in my half-drunk coffee. "And you can't smoke in a café anymore."

"No ... smoking is banned in all public places."

I raised an eyebrow. "Pubs?"

"Definitely not."

"Shit ..." I cleared my throat. "And ... and I'm now in 2016, you reckon?" As I uttered those words, the morning's events flashed around my brain. Akin to a chaotic pinball after the plunger had been yanked back, my thoughts were careering into bumpers, pinging back and forth. I was no *Pinball Wizard*, and *Who* I was now, forty years on from when I awoke this morning, was the burning question.

Until this point, the point of actually saying it, I'd tried to rationalise the completely mad situation I found myself in. Bang on the head, or a Blitzkrieg-styled remodelling of the town. However, it appeared that neither of those two events were responsible for my situation. The local planning office hadn't embarked on the mother-of-all town regeneration projects and, although I definitely hit my head on that concrete step, too much time had elapsed since that altercation to realistically explain these events.

So, perhaps I wasn't in a coma up at Fairfield General, but actually in 2016, forty years in the future.

"Jason. Jason," Beth shook my arm. "Are you okay? Chris, I think he's gone into shock. Shall I slap him? I'm not much good in these situations, but that's what they do in the movies, isn't it?"

Chris shrugged.

"You know, like when Andie MacDowell slapped Bill Murray."

"Beth, what are you on about?"

"You know, *Groundhog Day*, she slaps him loads of times."

"I don't think giving him a right hook is going to help. Don't you have to lay them in the recovery position or something like that?"

"Really? He's not having a fit. He just looks a bit glazed over." Beth leaned forward and peered into my eyes. I detected her hand waving back and forth. However, my mind was out of the traps, racing along, trying to work out how I would tackle the first hurdle on this new racetrack called the future.

"Well, I don't know, but he doesn't appear to be about to collapse." Chris tugged at her elbow, pulling her arm away from my face. "Beth, listen, this means that what Dad said was all true."

"It can't be, can it?" she hissed, settling back in her chair.

"What about what Buster Bloodvessel, Sebastian, said? Y'know, Dad telling stories about the future."

"I wouldn't take much credence from anything Buster says. The man's a perfectly built, killing machine. He's not likely to get an invitation from Mensa unless a bunch of academics need to hire a bouncer or a heavy to rip apart any member whose IQ drops below the required standard."

"Yeah, okay. But you got any better suggestions on how this bloke, the spit of Dad, has just floated in from the '70s?"

"Tell me again what Dad said? To be honest with you, when you told me after the funeral, I didn't really listen 'cos I thought you'd lost your bloody marbles."

As I vacantly stared across the café, or coffee shop as it apparently was now called, I listened to Chris recount his tale about his father's dying words.

"Okay. So, Dad said it was important that I listen to him and believe what he was about to say. I thought he was going to confess to cheating on Mum or that he had another child somewhere. For a moment, I feared he'd confess to being a murderer, like your uncle."

"Oh, please don't mention him. I might be related through blood, but he is nothing to do with me. Do not mention my real father's damn family!"

"Sorry, Sis. Anyway, as Dad croaked out his story, he wasn't unburdening a secret before leaving this world but, as I said, claiming to be a time traveller."

"Chris! Get on with it."

"Okay. All he said is that he was born in 1977. He time travelled from 2019 back to 1976, where he met Mum, adopted you and me after our mother, Carol, died, and took the place of some bloke with the same name. *Other* Jason, as he reckoned Mum and he used to call him," Chris waved his hand in my direction.

"And Mum believed all this bollocks?"

"So he said. Anyway, he reckoned he was involved in a car crash in 2019, died, and then woke up in 1976."

"I wish me and Phil hadn't gone down to Cornwall. I could have been there when Dad … you know."

Chris nodded. "It was all pretty sad to watch." He grabbed hold of his younger sister's hand when detecting her mood swing as he recounted their father's final moments.

Beth bowed her head and sniffed.

Chris wiggled her hand to encourage her to look at him. Beth nodded before using the heel of her other hand to wipe away a tear. "Alright?" he peered up at her as she nodded.

"I miss him."

"I know. I do too."

"Anyway, carry on."

"Right, where was I?"

"Dad recounting that he's a time traveller." She snorted a laugh and wiped the end of her nose with the back of her hand. "Christ, what bollocks."

Chris grinned. "Dad's favourite word."

Beth offered a smirk. "Go on, tell me the rest of this bollocks."

"Ah, yes. So, the bit about me checking out Cockfosters High Street and the Broxworth Estate after he died. Dad claimed he died in that crash in Cockfosters, and this *other* Jason bloke lived on the Broxworth."

"A crash in his BMW, I think you said."

"Yes. Dad claimed he was driving a BMW, a company car. He reckoned he died and came to in his Cortina in 1976."

"What company?"

"Oh, I've no idea. He didn't say … or maybe I'd glazed over at that point. Jesus, Beth, it was pretty hard going listening to Dad spout all that stuff."

"Yeah, Okay, okay, what next?"

"I'm getting there. Christ, you're just like Mum, always interrupting—"

"Well, you're just like Dad, never getting to the point."

Chris raised an eyebrow. "As I was saying, as Dad recounted his story, he said the Cortina must be kept safe and never driven."

"Why?"

"Well, I think he was convinced it's a time machine."

"Really? A 1974 Ford Cortina. Not exactly a DeLorean, is it!"

"No, I know. But Dad was really insistent about it."

"Okay, ignoring the fact that we have his lookalike sitting here," Beth shot me a look. "Where is Dad now, then?"

"What d'you mean?"

"Well, if he was living life in 2016, the time before he died in a car crash three years in the future, where is he?"

"Beth, Dad's dead."

"D'oh! Chris, I know! But he claimed to have been born in 1977, so in 2016, before the supposed crash in 2019, where is he?" Beth waved her arm about, scanning the coffee shop.

"You mean there should be a thirty-nine-year-old Jason Apsley living here now?"

"Yes!"

"Oh, well, I don't know. Perhaps that life has … changed, evaporated."

"Evaporated? What? All existence that Dad once knew just frittered away in a puff of smoke when he died in the future."

Chris shrugged. "Beth, I don't know, do I?"

"Christ, this is ridiculous. Anyway, what's the relevance to all this and him?" Beth shot me a look as she wagged her finger in my direction.

"Look, Dad was convinced that when he died, you know, this time, as in not in 2019, *other* Jason would appear."

"Why?"

"Paradox, or whatever. I don't know, all that time-travel shit. You know, you can't see yourself or be in the same place with your other self if you time travel."

"Oh … well, they do in the movies. Marty McFly saw himself. You remember the school dance?"

"Beth, that's the movies!" he hissed. "This is real life."

"Oh, yeah, course it is," she sarcastically huffed.

"Well, you know what I mean."

"Chris, this vacant gawping loony we have here isn't Dad!" Beth exclaimed, whilst thumbing over her shoulder in my direction.

"I know, I know, but that's what he said. *Other* Jason, as he called him, must have disappeared in 1976 when Dad landed in that year."

"Oh … what, like Dad time travels, takes his place, so he has to disappear because they can't co-exist?"

"Maybe, I don't know. Look, Beth, I really didn't think much about it because I assumed he'd lost his mind. Before I found this bloke, I assumed it was all bollocks. But Dad asked me to check those two places every day for thirty days to see if some bloke who looked like him turned up appearing to be a bit confused."

They both glanced at me before continuing with their hissed conversation.

"Beth, as I told you, he was insistent that I do this for him and not to think badly for saying such ridiculous things. If this bloke turned up, we would realise the truth. If he didn't show, he asked that we remember him as a loving father, not a lunatic."

"He was a loving father."

"He was. But listen to this. The one day he insisted I didn't miss when checking out those two places was today."

"Why?"

"Because Dad claimed he died on 12th August 2019 and landed the same day in 1976."

"So Dad assumed this *other* Jason would appear the same day? As in August the 12th, after he died?"

"I guess so."

"But it's 2016, not 2019."

"I don't bloody know, do I? But we have a bloke here who looks like Dad, claims to have the same name and wants us to believe that a few hours ago was living in 1976!"

"Oh—"

"And … and this bloke," Chris wagged his finger at me. "Reckons he owns a yellow Mark Three Cortina!"

"Dad's car? The car that's now in your garage."

The mention of my missing car hauled me from my thoughts. "Hang on, did you say you've got my car? The car that some bastard nicked this morning."

Beth and Chris exchanged a knowing nod before Chris leaned across the table. "Jason. First up, your car wasn't stolen this morning, as in 1976. And secondly, if that car, which Dad claims he woke up in back in '76, is your car, then I guess we will all have to agree that you, like our father, are a time traveller."

11

Who's on First?

"Well, is that yours?"

At least a minute had elapsed since Chris had pressed a button on a fob attached to his keyring, which, akin to some scene in a science-fiction film, raised the garage door to reveal my yellow Cortina.

The very same car that about an hour or so ago some bastard rear-ended before his accomplice larruped me a good'un. The licence plate was the same and, although false plates were reasonably easy to come by, I knew it was my car because of the identical half-crown-sized dent positioned dead-centre of the chrome bumper. A small dent and still visible despite whatever damage that clapped-out Bedford van had caused earlier this morning. However, was that altercation a few hours ago or, as Chris and his annoying sister were suggesting, forty years in the distant past?

"Jason?"

I glanced at Chris, who held his palms out, presumably waiting for me to confirm the ridiculous.

As was the trip in Chris's gadget-loaded car from the Broxworth into town, the ten-minute jaunt to his home was just as confusing. His house, an impressive building with an in-out driveway, seemed to have appeared along with the small estate where the old Belton's electronic components factory should be. Well, it was there yesterday because I'd driven past it.

Although the now missing corrugated-steel-clad factory lay derelict for some years, during Belton's heyday, back in the '60s, the firm employed a sizable chunk of the town's workforce. Colloquially known as *'Flunkers'* due to being the go-to place for most schoolkids who failed their exams and needed to earn a wage.

The factory's production lines had provided constant employment to meet the skyrocketing demands for electronic devices that claim to improve our lives. However, the company folded in the early '70s amidst the ever-increasing availability of more reliable and cheaper alternatives from Europe and the Far East. Also, the protracted collection of industrial disputes didn't help. Together, these two factors hammered down the final nails to the long-standing company's coffin lid.

When Chris had swung his gismo-infused beast of a car onto his drive, I thought the position of his house was probably somewhere on the lane which used to run down the side of Belton's to a secluded grove. An area favoured by young lovers, when their bedrooms in the homes of their conservative parents weren't an option, and for those embarking on illicit affairs and considered the cost of a hotel room too extravagant for the sake of a five-minute bunk-up on the back seat.

Although the lane bore no street name, everyone knew it as 'Lovers' Lane'. It was mooted by the town's folk that the parking area near the grove could claim to be the place of conception for the vast majority of those conceived on the wrong side of the blanket.

Anyway, along with just about everything else I remember from yesterday, Belton's old factory and Lovers' Lane no longer existed.

"Jason? Is it yours?" Chris repeated.

Mesmerised by the vision of my car, I failed to answer him, my mind whirring at the impossible that played out in front of me.

As Beth parked behind Chris's car, I wondered how many drivers had suffered verbal abuse from the scatty woman during that short trip.

In my youth, I'd been an avid reader of all things Arthur C. Clarke. Now, as I pondered how my car had ended up in the garage of a man with the same surname, who claimed his father time-travelled and took my place, I considered that if this were 2016, fifteen years on from 2001, the future didn't appear to be that different.

So far, I'd seen that portable telephone and a key fob which could open doors remotely. Although very different from my Cortina, cars still needed humans to drive them. Despite something Tattoo-Girl mentioned, I hadn't spotted any flying cars, and certainly nothing like Scaramanga's flying Matador Coupe. Also, apart from a somewhat impressively lifelike artificial voice emanating from the dashboard of Chris's car, advising him of a traffic jam ahead, there appeared to be a distinct lack of robots. That satellite navigation system, as Chris called it, wasn't exactly HAL 9000 or Andromeda.

Chris had stated that mankind had not colonised other planets. We didn't hold a space station outpost on the moon, and no other alien life forms had been discovered. So, I'd been left pondering what NASA had been doing for the last forty years, and perhaps Neil Armstrong's one small step wasn't such a giant leap for mankind as he'd suggested.

Nevertheless, although still struggling to get my head around time travel, Einstein's theories still held court in my brain.

"What's the matter with him?" asked Beth, as she joined us at the entrance to the garage.

"God knows. He's in that trance again."

"Did he say much on the way over? As you say, he's got that vacant look about him." She waved her hands in front of my eyes. "Earth calling Mr Weirdo from 1976. Are you with us?" she questioned, after dropping her waving arms, now peering into my eyes.

Stepping back, I huffed. "It looks like my car. I'll know for sure when I look inside."

"Amazeballs!"

"Why do you keep saying that?" I barked, causing her to hop backwards.

"Alright. Christ, keep your tits on. What's the matter with everyone today? I was only saying that it's all rather amazing, that's all. And let's face it, you claiming to have come from the past like some '70s throwback Doctor Who is pretty shamazing, wouldn't you say?"

I side-eyed her, not wishing to continue the conversation.

"Eh, Mr Weirdo, lost your tongue?"

"You're very annoying."

"I'm a woman. I'm supposed to be annoying. Well, that's what my husband says, God love him," she smirked, then turned to Chris. "What now, then?"

Chris shot me a look. "So, you think Dad's car is yours?"

"Yeah," I nodded. "And you're saying it's been in your garage for forty-odd years?"

"Well, Dad's garage, up until last year. Dad used to keep it in a lock-up on the other side of town. He got the local garage to tow it back to his house after someone smashed the lock and took it for a spin."

I offered him a confused frown, not understanding that statement. "Someone nicked it and brought it back?"

"Yeah," he chuckled. "Christ, that must be all of twenty years ago, I think. I was in my early twenties, so the early to mid-nineties, I reckon. Dad rarely went over there but just happened to nip over one day and discovered the padlock was broken. Amazingly, the car was still parked in the lock-up. The bloody thing was splattered with mud as if joy riders had taken it for a spin around a ploughed field."

"Then brought it back?"

"Yeah, they must have. I remember Dad being worried for the driver, which I remember thinking was a bit odd at the time."

"Why?"

"Well, rather than being angry, Dad seemed worried. Now, after what's happened, and Dad claiming he time travelled in it, I guess he was thinking that whoever took it for a spin may have time travelled."

Beth tutted and rolled her eyes.

"You remember that, surely?"

Beth shrugged. "Yeah, whatever."

"I don't get how my car could have ended up here … in your garage?" I mumbled, more of a question to my scientific brain than for either of them to answer.

"God, I can't get over how his voice is just like Dad's. It's a bit bloody creepy. You don't think …"

Chris shrugged before holding his hand up. "You're not suggesting—"

"Could he be Dad … somehow reincarnated?"

"What, as a forty-something bloke looking like he's just stepped out from the set of *Life on Mars?*"

"Oh, yeah, he does," she chortled. "*He looks as nervous as a short nun at a penguin shoot,*" she delivered in a deep voice. "D'you remember that bloke's quotes? God, they used to make me laugh. I remember Dad saying that twenty years after that series aired, he reckoned they would ban it because the jokes would be unacceptable in the future."

Chris shot Beth a look. "Beth."

"What?"

"Dad always said that. Didn't he?"

"Sorry, what are you talking about? Are we discussing the very un–PC Gene Hunt's quotes, or are we on another subject?"

"The future … y'know, like Buster Bloodvessel said earlier. How many times did Dad say, 'in the future'?" Chris performed the air quotes with his fingers. "Like Uncle Albert's 'during the war', Dad always said 'in the future'."

"Christ, did he ever! All the bloody time. We used to just roll our eyes at him."

Chris raised an eyebrow.

"Oh, I see … you think he was him telling us the future, as in the *actual future* … not Dad just being, well, dad-ish?"

"Oh, Beth, I don't know. But you should have heard him just before … you know. He was … well, almost as if possessed. And then what about the stuff he said about my holidays in 2004 and …"

Leaving them to discuss their father's ramblings, I stepped between them to inspect my missing car. The rubbing action of my hand back and forth across the back bumper confirmed this was my missing motor. However, why there appeared to be a lack of damage from my earlier rear-ending seemed somewhat bemusing.

Although I refused to believe the time-travel nonsense Chris spouted, I accepted it was reasonable to assume this Chris Apsley bloke hadn't stolen my car. Even if he had, he wouldn't then wait for me on the estate and drive me all the way across town to be reunited with it.

Also, despite him telling me his motor sported a three-litre turbocharged diesel engine which could achieve two-hundred-and-fifty-five BHP and over four-hundred pounds of torque – whatever the hell that was – I figured those statistics didn't offer enough time to complete that act and get back to T–wats store to wave that old snap in my face.

I pondered the thought that despite the world's lack of desire to continue the space race, future engineers had focused their energy on producing a decent diesel engine for cars.

Something I thought was only reserved for farm machinery, black cabs and trucks.

After sliding into the driver's seat and flipping down the sun visor, I wasn't overly surprised that my one-pound emergency note was missing. However, a car key dropped into my lap. "Jesus, do people still do that?" I muttered.

That said, my car was now parked in a locked garage situated in what appeared to be an affluent area, so I guess the chances of it being nicked were low.

Although the single key was clearly the one to my car, the transparent plastic fob containing a picture wasn't something I'd previously owned. The minuscule snap depicted a boy and a girl of secondary school age – the classic siblings' school photo. I shifted the rear-view mirror and held the picture aloft as I compared the image to Chris and Beth, who continued to yak away as they stood on the driveway.

Of course, they were much older, and that annoying 'amazeballs' woman no longer sported pigtails. However, their school blazers were purple, with the distinctive City School crest just about visible on the breast pockets.

I left the City School in 1949. Back then, the uniform was black. Although not sure why I knew this pointless fact, but the uniform changed to purple in 1972. So, if Chris and Beth were the two grown-up versions of the children in the picture, then there clearly was a problem with my timeline.

The glove compartment confirmed my *Wish You Were Here* cassette, along with about ten others, had also gone the way of that one-pound note. "Bastards," I mumbled, realising my favoured cassette tape, *Disraeli Gears by Cream,* had been amongst them. I was going to miss Ginger Baker's drum solos.

A quick peek under the passenger seat confirmed what I'd feared. My Philips cassette player, along with its black carry case, was also missing.

I prised out what appeared to be a yellow school exercise book that had wedged itself in the seat undercarriage mechanism. As I aimlessly fanned through the pages, I caught a whiff of that musty smell. A waft of stale vanilla that often emanated from old books. Although I'd always stored my cassette player there, I'd never previously noticed the book.

When lobbing it onto the passenger seat, I spotted the cover – *1994 to 1995* penned in blue ink – odd. Unsurprisingly, I noticed my black leather driving gloves were no longer there when performing a further rummage through the glove box. That space now contained just the car manual, a white envelope, and a collection of tax discs.

With the driver's door ajar, I could still hear brother and sister discussing their father. Although not listening in, it sounded like Beth was now doing most of the talking.

"Yak, yak, yak," I muttered. If I were now in the future, women talking too much hadn't changed over those years. "That's not fair," I mumbled, grabbing the manual and lobbing the collection of tax discs on the passenger seat. Although this Beth woman could give Lou Costello a run for his money regarding speed talking, my mother, God rest her soul, and my ex-girlfriend I'd left in South Africa didn't yak and didn't constantly trot out expletives, not to mention that damn word amazeballs.

"Amazeballs. Christ, what a stupid word," I muttered before noticing my handwriting penned in the margin on page 312 of the manual.

After returning to the UK in the spring, I'd picked up the Cortina at the Ford Garage in Luton. The chap in the dealership had impressed upon me the importance of choosing the correct engine oil, suggesting Castrol GTX, which Barry Sheene endorsed. And there it was. I'd actually written the names of the oil and that motorcycle racer in the margin. I recall that chap had then asked if I'd seen the new *Brut* advert with Henry Cooper and the blonde bird rubbing her hands all over Barry Sheene's bare chest. 'She could splash it all over me if she fancied,' he'd chuckled as we shook hands to seal the deal.

Despite all the evidence suggesting this was my Cortina, the collection of tax discs now lying fanned out on the passenger seat caught my eye and further confirmed the ridiculous.

Although sporting the correct registration, the blue one on top of the heap stated the expiry date of December 1977. A couple of hours ago, the tax disc stated December 1976. If this were still August 1976, which it should be, then a tax disc with that future date was – well, unless the post office had ballsed it up – impossible.

"So, it's your old motor, then?" Chris leaned down and stuck his head into the gap of the open door.

Still holding onto that future tax disc, I swivelled my head to be faced with the grinning couple as they peered down at me.

I nodded and pursed my lips.

"My God. Chris, d'you think Dad was actually telling the truth?"

"Well, he must have been. This bloke and Dad were … are, time travellers."

"Amazeballs!"

12

A Sound of Thunder

Whilst leaving me to fan through a collection of tax discs, including the one I'd purchased back in April, Chris and Beth continued where they'd left off when yakking away on the drive.

"Shit! What the hell are we going to do with him?"

"Oh, good point."

"I mean, technically, he doesn't actually exist, does he?"

"Well, he's there, right in front of our eyes. So, unless you and me have been puffing on some of your son's wacky gear, he deffo exists!"

"No, you know what I mean. He's landed from 1976, his flat is now occupied by some other woman, and he can hardly rock up to the school in a couple of weeks and start a job that he's forty years too late for the first day."

"Oh," Beth shrugged. "You'll have to put him up here."

"What? No way!"

"Well, I can hardly take him home and shove him in the spare room, can I? I think Phil might have something to say about that. Jesus, I can just imagine how that one will play out – oh, hi darling, how was your day. Guess what? I bumped into Buster Bloodvessel in Starbucks when I met this chap who just happens to be a doppelgänger for Dad from back in the '70s with the same name. I hope you don't mind, but I brought him home and said he could stay in the spare room. I thought we could adopt him. Oh, yes, and did I mention he's a time traveller? – Bloody hell, Chris, I don't think that's going to work, do you?" Beth thumped her hands on her hips and bulged her eyes whilst rocking her head from side to side.

"Err ... well, I think Megan might also have a bit of an issue if he stays here."

"Well, yeah, but we've got 'til the weekend. That gives us a few days to work out what to do with him."

"I think we're going to need a smidge longer than a couple of days," mumbled Chris. "Christ, can you imagine trying to convince anyone else that we've found a time traveller, and Dad, God rest his soul, was also a time traveller who just happened to ping from the future back to 1976? Bloody hell, Beth, we'll both be hauled off to the loony bin. Not to mention that Megan and Phil will be hot-footing to the divorce courts, suggesting we've both lost it." Chris's rant's rising inflexion suggested he was posing a question.

"Fuck it!" blurted Beth. "What the blue bollocks are we going to do?"

"You'd better read this," I interjected, waving a one-page hand-written note through the open car door.

Chris and Beth glanced down, Beth snatching the note from my grasp. "What is it?" she somewhat aggressively barked.

"Read it."

"Out loud," Chris demanded, as Beth scanned the letter.

"Dear Jason. Oh, it's a letter to Dad … to himself. It's his handwriting."

"It's my handwriting," I interjected. "A bit shaky, but it's definitely mine."

Beth and her brother shot me a questioning look. "You wrote it?" Chris asked.

"No, I didn't. It is in my handwriting, though. But there lies the problem."

"What?" they barked in unison.

"Look at the date."

Beth scanned to the top of the page. "October 2015. That's the month when Dad went into that care home."

"Where's this letter come from?" Chris shot at me as he dipped his head below the car's roof line.

"I just found it in the glove box."

"Oh, odd. Go on, Beth, what does it say?"

"Okay, here goes." Beth cleared her throat, glancing between her brother and me before reading aloud.

Dear Jason.

This is a somewhat odd letter to write. Penning a letter to my younger self is quite a tricky thing to do. Also, whether you'll actually receive this, well, who knows? However, you and I (although we are the same person) both know that strange things happen in that Cortina.

Anyway, to be honest with you, this is now my eleventh attempt at writing this damn letter. My other attempts have all gone the way of the shredder.

Anyway, let's move on from the ramblings of an old man. There is, of course, an enormous risk in penning this letter. If it were to fall into the hands of the wrong person, that could cause difficulties, to say the least. Chris and Beth still don't know who I am and where I come from, and as I enter my ninth decade, I'm still uncertain whether I will ever tell them.

For obvious reasons, I've not detailed future events because you already know them. However, certain information has come to the fore, and this is the reason for trying to contact you in the past.

You will remember the 12th August 2019, and specifically the news item on the radio as you (I) drove to work. I've not detailed them in this letter for the reason stated, but what was reported that day has happened again. I bent time in 1976, but as we know, time has a habit of pulling back to the laid-down path the future demands.

Now, whether that Cortina, still parked in our garage, can transport this letter through time – again, who knows? Also, if by chance this happens, I have no idea if you will receive this in time to act – but if you do – act, you must. Your daughter's life depends upon it.

As we both know, time travel is exclusive to just the three of us. April 1994, be ready to act. One of those time travellers will re-emerge under a pseudonym – you know what to do.

'Other' Jason still hasn't surfaced. Of course, as we both fear, I suspect he will after my death. Jess holds the key to ensure that, if this happens, 'other' Jason can continue where you and I've left off. However, unfortunately, I never got the

opportunity to prepare her for that day. I'm aware that this letter may seem vague, but as we share the same mind, I'm hoping you can read between the lines.

As we both know we're not the praying type, but I sincerely hope by sending this letter you can bend time and thus allow Jess to prepare.

Good luck to you (me).

Jason.

"What the …?" blurted Chris.

"Good God. Dad actually wrote to himself and posted the bloody letter in the glove box, expecting it to be posted back in time." Beth shook her head, glancing up at Chris. "Poor Dad must have lost his mind way before we realised."

Chris blew out his cheeks. "I really don't know what to make of that."

I waved the envelope at them. "It was in this, tucked inside the glove compartment."

Chris tentatively took the envelope and read the front—

To Jason from Jason

Strictly Private and Confidential.

(Chris and Beth. If you should discover this note, please resist the temptation to open it. As your father, I plead with you both to shred it without opening.)

"Oh, well, it's a bit bloody late for that! Mr Retro here has already torn it open. The genie's already out of the bottle."

"What does Dad mean … what did it say? Something about it's happened again?"

"Fuckerdedoda! D'you think Dad is referring to me or Jess?"

"What d'you mean?"

Beth glanced back at the letter, pointing to the text as she read it. "But if you do, act, you must. Your daughter's life depends upon it."

"My God, Beth. That letter said 1994!"

"Shit … you don't think?"

"Oh, Christ, I don't know. But it can't be a coincidence, can it?"

From my position in the driver's seat, I played head tennis between them as they appeared transfixed, open-mouthed, gawping at each other. Whilst waiting for someone to speak, I chewed through this morning's events – like one of my mother's famous plum duffs – it was heavy going.

Of course, none of it made any sense. My education had led me down the scientific path. The testing of theories against evidence obtained. What had transpired over the last few hours provided proof of either the supernatural or I'd suddenly become a loony. The latter seemed the most rational explanation.

As if some spiritual or a higher power decided to nudge my brain, a Red Admiral butterfly settled on the car's windscreen, directly in my eye line. The delicate creature twitched its wings back and forth as if waving to gain my attention.

Ray Bradbury's *A Sound of Thunder*, that short story about a time-travel safari hunt, drifted into my mind. Specifically, Eckels's boot with the dead butterfly stuck to the sole.

"Rihanna," I mumbled, as I closed my eyes to focus on the memory of that tattooed girl, now living in my flat, the one with that butterfly tattoo. The woman was probably in her late teens or early twenties. That butterfly tattoo had *'made in 1996'* inked beneath. When I'd first spotted it, I'd rightly dismissed that it couldn't be referencing the year. However, if this was 2016, she would be twenty – it all fitted.

"I have no idea if this has any relevance to what you two are talking about." I waved the child's exercise book I'd plucked from underneath the passenger seat. "It has 1994-1995 written on the front cover." Using it as a pointing stick, I jabbed the air back and forth between them. "I'll be straight with you both. I think I've come to the conclusion that I've suffered a brain haemorrhage, and in reality, I'm not really here. I reckon I'm actually on the slab in some operating theatre up at Fairfield General, and the anaesthetic is causing my mind to play out some vivid dream."

My scientific mind had settled on that explanation as the final reasoning, pushing ideas similar to those penned by my favourite science-fiction authors back to where they belonged – fantasy land.

Chris pursed his lips and nodded. "I guess I can see why you'd think that." He laid his hand on his chest. "But, Jason, I'm no apparition or a figment of your imagination." He pointed at Beth. "And my sister is very much here with us." He glanced at her, who nodded before offering an apathetic shrug of her shoulders.

"Yes, but you could say that in my dream, couldn't you?" I suggested, as I leaned out of the driver's seat and jabbed the rolled-up exercise book towards Chris, who appeared to be pondering my suggestion, before waving it in Beth's direction, that very act repeating the question at Beth.

In one swift movement, Beth released her right hand from her hip and slapped my face, Don Corleone style. Not a vicious slap, but followed up with something similar to that mafia boss's line – "Oh man up! So, you think you're dreaming, do you? Well, I guess you're not now, eh?"

"Jesus, Beth," blurted Chris.

"Thanks," I sarcastically replied. "Was that necessary?"

"I'm just trying to get you to realise you're not dreaming."

Whilst rubbing my cheek, and in fear of receiving another slap, I thought it best not to mention that I could still be dreaming that I'd just been whacked across the face by this Scarlet O'Hara-esque woman, who was really starting to grate on me.

"Yeah, thanks. If you just happen to think of something else that you feel the need to impress upon me, perhaps next time you could keep it to yourself," I suggested, pointing the rolled-up exercise book in her direction.

Beth shrugged, dramatically folded her arms and stuck her nose in the air. "There's no helping some people."

Chris reached out and took the exercise book from my hand. "Dad reckoned this car can transport you through time."

Beth tutted and dismissively shook her head.

Chris shot Beth a look before the roles reversed, and he jabbed the exercise book at me. "If what Dad was saying is correct, you were in that car this morning … well, 1976 version of this morning, when you travelled—"

"Time-travelled?" I interrupted, raising an eyebrow.

"Yeah, it seems that way. What I do know, this is 2016. If you're convinced that this morning was 1976, what other explanation can there be?"

I shot Beth a disparaging glare. "I'd suggest I'm dreaming in a comatose state, but I don't fancy another slap."

Beth raised her eyebrows at me, fortunately keeping her arms folded.

"Alright. Say I play along, just for one bizarre moment. I wasn't actually in the car when I supposedly time-travelled."

"You said you were driving off the estate, and someone drove into the back of you."

"Yeah, some douchebag in a Bedford van. I hopped out to have a word when some sleazeball punched … me." As I uttered the words, I realised that when I'd hopped out of the car, the Bedford van which had rear-ended me wasn't there. In that split second before being blinded by sunlight and that ring-festooned fist connected, I remember the fleeting surprise of the absence of the van that seconds before I'd spotted in the rear-view mirror.

"Jason?" quizzed Chris, presumably noticing that I seemed to have become lost in my thoughts.

I swallowed hard, the sound produced by my pharynx loud enough to haul me from my thoughts. "I think I was in the car," I mumbled.

Chris unrolled the exercise book. "Dad said …" he paused, glancing at his sister.

"What?" blurted Beth.

"I remember now. When Dad started to tell me about his time travelling," Chris paused again and glanced at the front cover. "He said I should have kept those damn exercise books."

13

The Siegfried Line

"What exercise books?"

"I don't know. As I said, I wasn't really listening," Chris mumbled as he perused the cover of the one in his hand. "I assume he means this."

"When Dad was delusionally ranting about all this, did he say book or books?"

"Err … books … I think," Chris replied, thumbing through the pages. "It's a list of events that happened in 1994 and 1995. A bit like a diary, but world events rather than personal stuff." Chris knitted his brows as he glanced up at his sister. "Why would he note down things like the collapse of Barings Bank? He's written rogue trader Mick Leeson with a question mark?"

"Who's he?"

"Well, Dad wrote his name down incorrectly because it was Nick Leeson, not Mick. He's the bloke who caused that bank to fail." Chris glanced back at the book, fanning through to a different page.

"Chris."

He glanced up at Beth. "What?"

"I think that book is a list of what will happen in the future, not a diary."

"Oh … you're suggesting he wrote this stuff before it happened?"

"Could be. If Dad time-travelled, then he'd know the future, wouldn't he?"

Chris waved the book at Beth. "So that's what he meant. Dad said he wished he'd kept the books. Presumably, to show me that he *was* telling the truth. Dad would have had books that detailed future events from 2016 to 2019."

"What about that one, then?"

"Well, I guess, somehow, he misplaced it when he destroyed the others. Anyway," Chris tapped his index finger on the front cover. "Recognise the handwriting?"

"Oh, Mum. Deffo, that's Mum's. Double underlining was her trademark. She even used to score a couple of lines under 'Love Mum and Dad' on our birthday cards, as if to emphasise the point. I think because we were adopted, she wanted us to be under no illusion that they both loved us."

Chris raised his eyebrows and nodded, the faint smile presumably caused by fond memories.

"Oh, d'you remember those signs she used to put out as reminders?"

"Signs?" Chris quizzed with knitted brows.

"Yeah. Y'know, the collection of cardboard signs, cue cards, if you like, to remind her to do something. She had one with '*Washing*', another with '*Freezer*', and she always double-underlined the words. I assume that was to remind her to get the washing in and defrost something for tea."

Chris snorted a laugh and shook his head.

"I remember Uncle George wrote '*Hang Out Your*' and '*On The Siegfried Line*' on either side of '*Washing*'."

"Oh, God, yes," Chris chuckled, "And Mum got the right hump."

"And on the other one, after '*Freezer*', he wrote '*Jolly Good Fellow*'," chortled Beth.

"Yeah, he did," Chris nodded. "I'd forgotten about them. I suppose that was what you used before the Post-it Note. God, I don't half miss her. I know I'm closer to fifty than forty, but everyone needs their mum."

"I know. I miss her so much. Even though she was closer to you than me."

"What?" Chris furrowed his brow. "What d'you mean?"

"I was a Daddy's girl, and you a Mummy's boy," she shrugged. "That's just how it was."

"Well, I have no idea where you get that idea from."

"You're having a laugh! Christ, you know damn well that Mum always defended you over me!"

"Bollocks, did she!"

"She bloody did. Every time we argued, Mum would take your side."

Chris blew a raspberry. "That's bollocks. Anyway, you could get away with blue-bloody murder with Dad. Tip your head on your side and whine that I done something, and he would become putty in your hands."

"Fuckerdedoda, did he! Anyway, that's probably—"

"Enough!" I bellowed, effectively halting their bickering. Beth and Chris shot me a look as I swung my legs out of the car. "Remind me, how old are you both?"

Chris and Beth exchanged a glance, both shrugging their shoulders.

"Forty-six."

"Thirty-nine."

"Okay. So, although in my short few hours here, wherever the hell this is, I accept there seems to have been some technological advances since the mid-seventies. Your motor, those telephones, TV beamed from out of space. But … it appears the human race has degenerated. You two stand there bickering like Janet and John whilst I—"

"Who?" chimed in Beth.

"Janet and John. You know, the children's books."

"I have no idea what you're … oh, hang on. Chris," she chortled. "D'you remember when Wogan used to do the Janet and John series on the breakfast show on Radio 2. What was it … *Wake Up to Wogan*? Dad used to piss himself laughing. I remember Mum saying it was smutty with all those innuendoes."

I shot the palm of my hand up at Chris as he opened his mouth to reply. "No!"

Chris gave a reasonably acceptable impersonation of a goldfish as I bashed on. "What I'm saying is that you both appear not to have grasped the situation. Continually trotting out stupid words like 'amazeballs' and 'fuckerdedoda', along with bickering about which parent loved you the most like a couple of spoilt brats. If you'd have lived through the bloody war, you'd have a bit more backbone about you both."

"During the war," sniggered Chris, before dropping the smirk when noticing my glower.

"If my car is some modern-day version of H. G. Wells's time machine, then bickering about your parents isn't helping my situation." I scrubbed my hand over my face. "Christ, am I actually saying this?" I muttered.

Chris pursed his lips and inspected the garage floor whilst Beth, now with her hands on her hips, rolled her eyes around the rafters.

"Right. So, what you're both saying … your father died in the future, and time travelled back to 1976, where he took my place. If that's the case, where the hell have I been for forty years?"

Whilst holding my palms open in a questioning style, I shot glances between them. Both didn't respond, instead choosing to continue to inspect the floor and garage roof.

"Okay, let's just say, for argument's sake, that this *is* 2016. Your father has just passed. I've now landed from my forty years of living in oblivion to take his place, and my second-hand 1974 Mark Three Cortina is a time machine."

Still with his head bowed, Chris shot me a look whilst I continued.

"Also, if that letter is to be believed, your father wrote to himself and placed that letter in this *time machine,*" I uttered those two words with more than a hint of sarcasm. "Telling his younger self about some repeated issue which happened in the future that has re-happened in the past. Something involving my daughter, Jessica. So, how am I doing so far?"

Beth cleared her throat, seemingly satisfied that the garage roof appeared okay, and offered a whimsical smile. Although not a verbal response, it was better than a slap.

"Where's Jess then?"

Beth shot Chris a look. Something in her expression suggested all was not good with my daughter in the future. Well, my future – her past – if this time-travel malarkey was to be believed.

"Well? Is someone going to answer me, or are you both going to carry on staring at each other like a couple of gormless nitwits?"

Beth squatted down on her haunches, clamping my hands in hers. "In 1994, something happened to Jess." Beth hesitated, glancing up at Chris and then back to me.

"Go on."

"On the 6th April 1994, Jess left her home to pick up her daughter, Faith, from college."

"Faith?"

"Technically, your granddaughter, I guess," chimed in Chris.

"Oh," I muttered, somewhat bemused that I could be a grandfather at forty-two. On the other hand, I guess it was mathematically possible. Being quick with maths, I deduced this Faith would be a teenager in 1994, thus born in the late '70s. So, although this morning in 1976, I wasn't a grandfather, a few hours later in 2016, it appeared I was.

"She never turned up."

"Who?"

"Jess never turned up to collect Faith."

I glanced up at Chris and then back at Beth. Although continuing to firmly clamp my hands in hers, she now bowed her head, leaving me staring at her hair.

"Where did she go?"

Beth raised her head, her face streaming with tears. "We don't know. Jess left her home at half four. Traffic cameras place her on the Haverhill Road at a quarter to five."

"Traffic cameras? What, like police speed guns?"

"No, Jason. Everywhere, well, nearly everywhere, is covered by CCTV," added Chris.

"Orwell's 1984," I muttered.

"Big Brother watching us all."

"Is that what it's like now? The state watching over your every move?"

"Not like Orwell's version of the future. But, yes, there are cameras everywhere you look."

I glanced back to the driveway, trying to spot if we were being watched.

"Oh, not on residential housing estates," Chris added when spotting my line of sight.

"Right. So, what happened? If everywhere is covered by CCTV, presumably she got picked up on another camera?"

Beth shot Chris a look whilst releasing her left hand to wipe away the tears.

Chris nodded, presumably taking her nonverbal request to continue with the story. "What Beth is saying … Jess's car was caught on camera on the Haverhill Road, but as she drove out into the countryside," Chris paused. "There aren't many cameras out that way."

"She was never seen again?"

Chris pursed his lip and offered a light shake of his head. "Jess has been a missing person since 1994 ... twenty-two years."

14

Public Eye

Unlike the man who Beth and Chris referred to as their father, this Jason Apsley bloke who apparently looked and sounded just like me, the very man who'd stolen my life and sent me off on a forty-year time-travel excursion, I hadn't been the paternal type.

Of course, I wasn't proud of shirking away from my fatherly responsibilities. However, at the time, when only twenty-two, I wasn't ready for fatherhood. On the other hand, my girlfriend had yearned for us to settle down and play happy families.

Notwithstanding the irresponsibility of my actions, I'd not wanted to become a parent at such a young age. With my National Service behind me and focusing on my studies, the possibilities in the mid-fifties seemed endless. The country was entering the economic boom years and smack in the middle of the baby boom, which we had unintentionally added to. Rationing was almost a distant memory; the regeneration of the bombed-out cities was now bowling along with new housing estates springing up in the suburbs like a plague of rabid triffids gobbling up the greenbelts; the middle classes were rushing out to grab television sets and cars, and nearly everyone had access to a telephone. Well, ones that were connected to the exchange, not that new-fangled thing Chris had shown me.

As our university years came to a conclusion, my girlfriend harboured a clear vision of our future – namely, her, I, and Jessica moving into one of the newly built council houses; me with a pipe, her with a pinny on keeping house, already with her eye on a Bendix twin-tub washer – safe to say, it wasn't my idea of how I imagined my future.

1956, the dawn of the post-war, new modern world, rock and roll and Elvis Presley, the emergence of the first self-service supermarkets and nuclear power stations. A truly modern era, and only a year from Macmillan's claim that we'd never had it so good, or something like that.

However, despite the good times we were experiencing, the threat of war was upon us again. The Americans had developed the hydrogen bomb and, at around that time, the government of the day were shovelling out pamphlets on how to survive a nuclear war.

The Cold War and arms race intensified as the next two decades unfolded, despite my ex-girlfriend's vehement protesting at the 'Ban the Bomb' demonstrations. I'd heard on the grapevine that she'd become a leading light in the movement. The ever-increasing stockpile of bigger and more destructive weapons led to those suggested precautions of *'Take Cover'* heralding a certain pointlessness. The term *mutually assured destruction* had never been so apt.

So, there we were in 1956, me, the scientist with the world my oyster. Despite her fetish for a twin-tub and the fact that we'd produced a baby girl, my girlfriend had latched onto every opportunity to protest. It's safe to say she'd become an enthusiastic activist, protesting against this, that and everything. With a first in Law under her belt, it made for a formidable combination. We harboured very different views, which only served to add pressure to the relationship. You could say she, the Katie Morosky character and me, the Hubbell Gardiner.

Although I'd been an avid supporter of capital punishment in my youth, probably due to agreeing with the vast majority who wished to see the Nazis hang in Nuremberg, my time in South Africa changed my perspective. The apartheid system only served to disproportionately send innocent black men to their deaths. However, in 1956, I held very different views.

Why I recall this was probably that issue served as a headliner of mine and my girlfriend's differences of opinions, of which there were many. I recall how she, less than a month after the birth of our daughter, had taken our babe-in-arms with her to stand outside Holloway Prison to join the masses when protesting against the hanging of Ruth Ellis.

Anyway, putting one of our many arguments to one side, there was no denying that I'd let her down and run away from my responsibilities. Over the last fifteen years, I'd regularly popped back to the UK to see my parents, who'd both now passed. During those fleeting visits, I'd often been tempted to try to find my daughter. However, I'd never succumbed to that temptation, always finding some excuse, like a visit to White Hart Lane to watch Spurs play. As the years drifted by, along with watching Spurs after the heady days of the early-sixties successes, the yearning desire to find Jessica faded.

When permanently relocating back to good-old Blighty in the spring, again, the idea of finding my twenty-year-old daughter often nudged into my brain. However, I'd always managed to push those thoughts away, probably through fear of rejection, which would have been fair enough.

Then, a couple of months back, after a trip to London, I spotted her mother when hopping off the train at Fairfield Station. Despite the passage of nearly twenty years elapsing since the day I'd walked out on her, I instantly recognised my ex.

After taking great care not to be spotted, creeping along like Frank Marker from *Public Eye,* I followed her home. I'd even got as far as stepping up to the front door with a raised hand ready to knock before thinking better of it. The TV enquiry agent and I had a certain affinity, without the regulation mac, but in our forties, single and intelligent. Although I benefited from a sunny disposition, unlike his dour persona. That said, after the last hour or so, I now struggled to muster up any positivity and now questioned my intelligence or even my sanity.

Now, sitting in my time-travelling car, and if Chris and Beth were to be believed, forty years in the future, I'd missed my chance. Not that I held any burning desire to see my ex, but my dithering about making contact with my daughter, Jessica, meant that I was too late. Apparently, twenty-two years too late.

Still holding onto my hand with a firm grip, whether for balance or comfort, Beth took up the story of my daughter's twenty-two-year-old missing person status.

"The police weren't that interested to start with. They just said Jess must have gone to stay with friends, and they suspected she'd show up a day or two later. But we knew …" Beth paused, allowing me to jump in.

"What about these cameras? Surely she'd have been spotted at some point."

"That's twenty-odd years ago. Although everywhere is now plastered with the damn things, they weren't so in the '90s," chipped in Chris, who now rested his backside on the nearside wing of the Cortina. His paunch suggested he wasn't the sporty type. Instead, he probably spent most of his day perched behind a desk, shuffling paperwork or asking his secretary to take a letter. As he shifted his weight, I could detect the car's suspension groaning.

Beth continued. "Mum, Dad, well, pretty much everyone, searched for months … years, even. We have an entire website dedicated to finding her. Up until even perhaps five years ago, we'd regularly received emails claiming they'd seen her in far-flung places. One bloke reckoned he's spotted her checking into a hotel in Bangkok."

"Not the Hilton, of course," chuckled Chris, which morphed into an apologetic whine when Beth shot him a look. "Sorry, it was just a joke."

"Not really a joking matter, is it?"

"Sorry," Chris held up his hands in a placating gesture.

"I'm a bit lost. What's the joke?"

"Oh, forget it," Beth bit back. I figured she wasn't having a go at me but rather the continued frustration with her brother, who appeared suitably chastised.

"What's an email, then?" I threw in to break Beth's glare.

"Shit me, was the '70s really that backward?" Beth puffed her cheeks out. "For the want of a better word, it's electronically sent letters, like …" she paused.

"A telegram, without the need for it to be delivered, or printed, or the word stop after each sentence," chimed in Chris.

"Nothing like it, then?" I suggested.

"No, not really. Look, Jason, the point Beth is making. We, as a family, have tried everything to find her."

"What about her husband? I'm assuming she was married?"

"Yes. And he's never given up. He actually flew out to Bangkok as soon as that bloke said she'd been spotted."

"Oh. Obviously, it wasn't Jess?"

"No, false alarm like every other sighting. Mum and Dad put up a mahoosive reward for any information that would lead to finding her. A hundred grand, no less."

"Pounds? English pounds?"

"Yes … is there another sort?"

"Egyptian. Although, that would only convert to a couple of grand. And Cypriot, of course."

"I'm pretty sure they've got the Euro now," Chris interjected.

"Who has?" batted back Beth.

"Cyprus. Megan and I holidayed in Paphos last summer. I'm certain that they have the Euro."

"Cyprus … that's a bit dodgy for a holiday, what with the Turkish invasion."

Chris furrowed his brow. "Oh, you're still on '70s time," he chortled. "No, Cyprus is a popular holiday destination these days, both North and South." Chris rubbed his chin and pursed his lips. "I'm not sure if the North has the Euro, or the Turkish Lira, though."

"What's the Euro?"

"Oh, that's the new currency that most of Europe uses. It came in … well, the back end of the last century. 1999, to be precise. Britain decided not to join the single currency and kept the pound."

"We're still in the Common Market, though?"

"Well, technically, yes, at the moment. That newspaper headline I showed you this morning. Y'know the headline, May saying Brexit means Brexit. Well, that was the Prime Minister saying she would ensure that the government would adhere to the referendum and take the UK out of the EU.

"EU?"

"European Union … Common Market as you knew it. I work at the Foreign Office and, I can tell you, it's bloody bedlam in there at the moment—"

"And this May is a woman … Prime Minister?"

"Fucktangle, Fucker-de-fuck! What the bollocks are you two twittering on about? We're discussing Jess, not the history of the bleeding European Union."

I exchanged a glance with Chris. Although keen to hear more, I could tell he, like I, had realised his potty-mouthed sister made a valid point, despite her odd expletives.

"So, as I was saying, before you dragged the conversation off to sodding Brexit, something you and I totally disagree on, I might add." Beth wagged an accusing finger at Chris. "You know it will be your fault when the country goes tits up. Phil can't believe you and Megan were stupid enough to fall for all that bollocks Boris and Farage trotted out."

Chris waved his hands, appearing to dismiss her statement. "Move on. I think we've had our fill of that bloody argument."

"Yes, well, I'm just saying, eh!" Beth tutted at Chris before turning to me. "So, as I was saying, Mum and Dad put up the reward. And yes, it was a hundred grand in sterling."

"Bloody hell, serious cash," I mumbled. Although the content of my missing safety deposit box held a significant haul of diamonds, I considered a hundred grand was not what the average family could lay their hands on. Nevertheless, if a packet of smokes cost thirteen quid, then maybe it wasn't such a significant amount.

"That's what we said. Of course, we had no idea where the hell they planned to get their hands on a hundred grand."

"I think I might," I muttered.

"Sorry?" quizzed Beth, shooting a look at Chris.

"Did your father ever mention a safety deposit box?"

Beth and Chris exchanged a shrug. "No," they replied in unison. "Why?" quizzed Chris.

"No reason."

At this stage, as in not totally convinced whether I'd broken all laws of relativity and somehow managed to time travel in a mass-produced saloon car, the contents of my missing safety deposit box needed to remain on a strict need-to-know basis. That said, I'd come to accept that it was unlikely to still be in situ in the basement of that café called Star-something-or-other. So, the question in my mind – had their father benefited from my slightly dubious acquisition of a bag of flawless diamonds? As I mused over this disturbing possibility, Chris took up the story.

"I'm afraid that Jess, our half-sister, your daughter, is … probably dead. Even if she's not, we've got more chance of finding Lord Lucan.

I shot Chris a look. "Christ, they never found him?"

"Lucan?"

"Yeah. The toff who bludgeoned the nanny a couple of years ago."

"Forty years, at least. And no, like Jess, he was never found."

Copying an act that Beth liked to perform, I puffed out my cheeks. Beth, now probably feeling she no longer needed to hold my hand, hopped back into a standing position before plucking up the letter from where she'd earlier placed it on a shelf next to an assortment of tins of paint.

"Hang on … this letter suggests Dad discovered what happened to Jess. Last year, he must have known something."

"He's suggesting that in 1994," Chris paused. "Read that bit about someone turning up."

Beth scanned the letter. "Err … oh, here it is," she tapped the page as she read aloud. "As we both know, time travel is exclusive to just the three of us. April 1994, be ready to act. One of those time travellers will re-emerge under a pseudonym – you know what to do."

"Three? Three, time travellers."

"That's what he's written."

"Dad hoped that letter would make it back to 1994, so his younger self could prevent something from happening.

Something which he became aware of in 2015," Chris affirmed with a wag of his finger. As he shifted his weight again, the bonnet offered a loud ping.

"Yes, but the letter never made it back, did it? Which is no sodding surprise. I mean, the idea that the glove box of his old Cortina is a time portal is bloody ridiculous."

"I don't get it. If it had made it back to 1994, and Dad back then acted upon what Dad of last year is asking of him—"

"You've lost me, dear brother."

Chris shifted further forward, my poor car groaning under the strain. "If Dad, back in the '90s, had read this letter and stopped Jess disappearing, what would have happened to now … as in right now? Jess is still missing."

"Oh, I don't bloody get it." As Beth jabbed the letter at Chris, I snatched it from her, rereading it whilst she continued. "We were there when Jess disappeared. If Dad of yesteryear had managed to stop that happening, would Jess suddenly reappear like nothing had happened?"

"Dunno," Chris shrugged.

"The grandfather paradox," I mumbled, causing Beth and Chris to shoot me a look. "It's a theory of time-travel paradox. It was first discussed twenty or thirty years ago. We used to debate it at university, but I left the group because it was becoming ridiculous. You see, I'm more interested in physics and the—"

"Great!" Beth sarcastically interrupted. "Not wanting to appear rude. But what the blue bollocks has your debating society from university got to do with this?" She bent forward, hooking her hair around her ear as she glowered at me.

"Closed timeline curves."

"Really?" barked Beth.

"God, you're aggressive."

"You've not seen anything yet if you think this is aggressive. Christ, Mr Retro Man, spit it out in plain bloody English if you please."

"It's in her DNA," chuckled Chris. "You should meet her biological family. I met her grandmother once, not something I'm likely to forget."

Beth reeled around, stepping towards Chris. The open car door acting as a barrier to stop her from slapping him. "Christ almighty, you can bloody talk. You don't even know who your bloody real father is! And if our biological mother is anything to go by, I can't imagine he was exactly an upstanding member of society. Jesus, Chris—"

"Beth. Beth, I'm sorry, I'm sorry," Chris leaned back, causing the car's bonnet to ping as his weight shifted. "I was just trying to lighten the mood."

Beth wagged her finger at her brother over the car door. "Lighten the sodding mood! It might have escaped your attention, but we're discussing our missing sister. Not to mention the slight issue that we have Mr Retro Time Traveller here with no sodding idea what to do with him. And … and, I have a ten-year-old boy who's spent all day chundering at summer camp and needs his mother!"

"Err … can I interject?" I tentatively asked, conscious I was in slapping range of the deranged woman.

"What?" she barked, glowering down at me.

"I was," I paused, shaking my head at the ridiculous suggestion my brain had conjured up. "I was going to mention alternative timelines."

Presumably, now considering it was safe to nudge forward, Chris slid his backside along the wing and folded his arms on top of the open door. "You think, if Dad had read this letter and intervened in 1994, Jess would be okay and living in some alternative timeline? Meaning, in that alternate world, we are all together again?"

"Well, as much as time travel to the past is completely impossible, for a whole host of reasons that I won't go into right now, but yes, that's what I'm suggesting."

"But you're here … with Chris and me in 2016. So, you can shove your physical impossibilities theories up your bum. And despite Jess still being missing, you being here is one hell of a clusterfuck." Beth raised that pencilled-on eyebrow at me. I imagined her son and husband were familiar with this expression when Beth felt the need to sermonise and hammer home her opinions upon them.

I could only assume that her husband, Phil, was either a saint and happily existed under this curmudgeonly woman's thumb, or their household was akin to a war zone that would probably rival the current poor relations between North and South Vietnam. Although, presumably, if this was 2016, that war had now concluded.

"Jason," Chris paused as I glanced up at him. "Beth makes a good point."

"What, shove my theories up my arse?"

"No … today is precisely forty years after you woke up on the morning of the 12th of August 1976. And it is one hell of a clusterfuck."

15

Vanishing Point

A couple of months ago, well, no, make that forty years and a couple of months ago, I'd got chatting to this woman in the Bell Pub in town. Not my usual drinking hole, but I'd planned to meet an old mate who didn't show.

When propping up the bar, I got talking to this girl who was enjoying a night out with a group of girlfriends. I'd given her the eye as she swished her long-layered hair from side to side, expertly swaying in rhythm to the Bay City Rollers that some knob had selected on the jukebox. The actual song title completely escapes me, what with me being more of a Led Zep type of bloke.

Anyway, she caught my eye, and we got chatting. Apparently, I looked like her heartthrob, Noel Edmonds. Although she was probably a good fifteen years younger than me, I think after I'd trotted out the line that I'd lived in South Africa and mined diamonds for a living, she probably thought I might be worth getting to know. Well, let's face it, diamonds are a girl's best friend, according to the captivating Carol Channing and the glamourous Marilyn.

One thing led to another, and we agreed on a date. The late showing of *Jaws* at the ABC in town. As it turned out, a particularly good choice because Sarah, yes, that was her name, Sarah, clung to me for dear life throughout the showing. However, despite the closeness we forged in those two cinema seats, we didn't make it to the third date.

I guess that despite my exciting tales of sparkly stones over a steak and glass of Yugoslavian Riesling at the local Berni Inn, the age gap between us was obvious. Despite her Bardot-esque appearance, her constant chatter and infatuation for the Scottish pop band only served to confirm we were not meant for each other. It was definitely a case of *Bye Bye Baby*.

Now, what relevance has this? Well, that movie score by John Williams stuck with me. As I slumped back in the driver's seat, pondering what the hell I was going to do with my new life, now living forty years in the future, that haunting music filled the garage space.

"Really? Bloody hell, Chris, is that your sodding ringtone?"

"What's wrong with it?" he scowled at his sister whilst patting his pockets before grabbing his telephone-cum-torch-cum-whatever from his standard-issue Civil Service suit jacket pocket. Apart from the shrinking size of lapels and a somewhat conservative shirt collar, it appeared office attire hadn't significantly changed from my time.

"Oh, bollocks, it's work. I'm gonna have to take it. It'll be some sodding crisis that no other bugger's capable of sorting out," Chris muttered, as he padded back to the driveway, closely followed by Beth, who either was planning on listening in on his conversation or just didn't fancy my company.

After scrubbing my hands down my face, I repositioned the rear-view mirror to keep an eye on my new best friends. Whilst animatedly pointing back in my direction, Beth appeared to berate Chris. I shook my head in dismay as I watched Chris flail his hand at her, clearly frustrated by her interruptions.

"Fuckerdedoda, Chris. We have a crisis of our own here. Just tell them to get on with it, so we can work out what to do with him," she hollered, while Chris once again gestured for his sister to back away.

"Fuckerdedoda," I muttered, pondering if that was even a word. I slotted that odd letter in my jacket pocket and plucked up the key ring to study the picture of the two children depicted in their school uniform.

The girl was clearly Beth. A pretty girl who'd morphed from childhood into a bit of a looker with a vicious mouth that could strip the flesh from your bones in one sitting – a human version of that Great White, if you like. The boy, again, clearly Chris, appeared athletic, toned, sporting a chiselled jaw. Something had clearly gone awry there, which the suspension of my time-travelling car could attest to when having to support his lard-arse for the best part of half an hour.

If I could just suspend belief for a moment, I wondered about alternative timelines. Of course, that letter – intended to be fired back through time via a portal that just happened to be positioned in the glove compartment of my car to the man who'd taken my life – simply had to be a fake. And if that were to be the case, why the charades from them two? Also, if they were acting, they were both good enough to hold Equity cards.

I glanced again in the rear-view mirror, spotting their continued sibling squabble. Beth now trying to grab Chris's portable telephone. "Jesus," I tutted, shaking my head.

So, alternate timelines. Could that chap, Jason Apsley, have received the letter in 1994 and just decided to leave it in the car for safekeeping? Could my daughter, Jessica, be alive and well, living in a parallel universe? A hell of a question that my old chums in that pointless debating society would have foamed at the mouth about given the opportunity.

If that could happen, as in the reality of closed timeline curves, would this Beth woman, as a result of her half-sister never going missing, be – what was the word – normal, yes normal, that covered it. Chris's athletic, youthful appearance in that school snap suggested the man hadn't maintained his health. Perhaps, in that other timeline, he'd taken a different trajectory and regularly walloped a squash ball around?

One thing is for sure, despite my reluctance to suspend belief and my scientific mind demanding an explanation for this morning's events, I couldn't wait around for these two oddballs to make decisions about my life.

After closing the car door and thumping down the lock button, I shimmied around and checked all the doors' locks were depressed before ramming the key in the ignition.

"One small step," I muttered, before checking Beth and Chris weren't in my path.

Chris had mentioned that his father had stipulated that the car must never be driven. So, if he'd complied with his father's request, there was a real chance that my forty-year-old motor wasn't going to start. I could safely assume the battery would be as dead as a dodo or even disconnected. With my hand poised on the key, I pondered if I should pop the bonnet and check. However, that would take too much time. Anyway, when I twisted my wrist, I'd find out.

After taking a deep breath, I released the handbrake, pulled the choke out about an inch, and turned the key.

Nothing.

"Sod it," I muttered.

Another furtive glance in the rear-view mirror confirmed Chris and Beth remained in position. Although Chris appeared to be no longer taking that call from his office, their joint finger-wagging and hand-waving gestures suggested they disagreed on their next move. Going by the way that Beth appeared to be advancing and Chris's backward steps, she seemed to be unleashing her preferred vitriol of invectives.

The thought of spending any more time with these two spurred me into action. Whilst, unusually for me, offering up a silent prayer, I prepared for a second attempt to start my motor. After half a dozen pumps of the accelerator, coupled with a hearty tug on the choke, I twisted the key. The engine fired and raced as I continually pumped my right foot.

"Amazeballs," I chuckled.

However, as I shifted into reverse, my path now appeared blocked by Chris and Beth who'd bolted towards the car. When both materialised through the cloud of blueish smoke that cloaked the garage opening, I wondered if Scotty had shifted the *energize* dial.

The vision in my rear-view mirror depicted them waving and hollering at me, none of which was audible over the roar of the engine. "Come on, move," I hissed. Although not a prayer, my request was answered when they scooted to either side of the car. Beth repeatedly yanked at the driver's door handle whilst furiously slapping her hand on the window. Ignoring her pleading for me to open the door, I continued to pump my right foot to drown out her string of expletives. Most of which I detected were her favoured made-up ones beginning with that four-letter word.

With an equal measure of concern, Chris copied his sister as he slapped both hands on the passenger window. His pained expression reminded me of Dustin Hoffman's demented performance in the finale of *The Graduate*. However, he vociferated my name as opposed to *Elaine*. I guess it was fairly safe to assume he wasn't attempting to halt a marriage but to prevent me from driving what he believed to be a time machine. Despite their protestations and now with a clear driveway behind me, I needed to ascertain if their father's claims were correct.

Would I time travel or just shoot out onto the road that had replaced 'Lovers' Lane'? Well, I was about to find out. "Here goes for nothing," I muttered, wondering where I'd end up before flooring the accelerator. In true Kowalski style, although in a 1974 Cortina and not a supercharged 1970 Dodge Charger, I wheel-spun from the garage, heading to perhaps my *Vanishing Point*.

Notwithstanding the cloud of smoke, a mixture of tyre burnout and engine-oil-infused exhaust fumes, I only managed to reverse about thirty feet across the drive before coming to an abrupt halt.

The reason for the Cortina's sudden lack of movement wasn't because I'd applied the brake. I hadn't suddenly been distracted by a vision of Gilda Texter, who that girl, Sarah, from the Bell Pub reminded me of, appearing nude whilst riding a motorbike, a scene from that movie that would stick in the mind of any red-blooded male. No, my stationary position was caused by a similar event that halted Kozlowski's interstate speeding trip. Not a headlong sprint into a couple of bulldozers, but more of a rear-end altercation with a dustcart that had pulled up and blocked the drive. Unfortunately, the smoke emanating from my wheel spin had temporarily obscured my view behind me. Now I suspected that the rear end of my Cortina sported significantly greater damage than a half-crown-sized dent in the bumper.

Whilst wincing because of the pain caused by my nose's collision with the steering wheel, I involuntarily snorted in lungfuls of the unmistakable stench of burning rubber. As I gingerly lifted my head, concerned about the extent of the damage to my neck from the whiplash after the rather abrupt curtailment of my escape, my blurred vision spotted Beth and Chris hot-footing through the cloud of smoke towards me.

Before the inevitable slip from consciousness, for the second time today, I became more than a little concerned at the glow and flicker from the flames which danced in the rear-view mirror. As my brain circuitry faltered and my disorientated vision fixated on the conflagration that appeared to have engulfed the boot lid, I detected a loud boom. Similar to when I'd cracked my head in that stairwell, darkness once again took hold.

16

Bloody Friday

When rather groggily coming to in that stairwell earlier today, probably because Rihanna, or whatever her damn name was, had hollered at me, I'd initially assumed I was dead. A reasonable assumption to make, I venture. However, when I'd opened my eyes, clearly, I wasn't.

Now, as I gingerly ratcheted up my eyelids after presumably suffering a blackout in my Cortina following the altercation with the dustcart, the scene in front of me appeared very different. No tattooed-metal-piercing-festooned Rihanna stood before me. Instead, I was faced with nothing – pitch black, total darkness.

When involuntarily placing my hand on my heart, the slow beat indicated I was breathing, as did the slightly panicky intake of air. I could wiggle my toes and a quick fumble about suggested I was still sitting in the car. Overall, a good start.

However, although alive and not quite at Corporal Jones's level, panic set in when the realisation came to the fore that the reason for the war-time styled blackout was probably due to the fact that I was now blind.

Whatever had happened when I'd smacked into that truck, going by the total lack of any illumination, it was reasonable to assume one of my sustained injuries had resulted in the loss of my sight. To quote my adopted friends, today was turning out to be one hell of a clusterfuck.

Whilst silently panicking about my future, specifically the low odds of a fulfilling life for a blind, potless, homeless man living in the future, my pupils dilated. As they adjusted to the lack of light, peculiar, murky shapes emerged from the indistinct, nebulous scene through the windscreen.

The inside of the car became visible, and the greyish shapes in the middle distance morphed into a line of trees. On a positive note, it appeared I hadn't been blinded. However, after that altercation with a dustcart, I'd blacked out before lunchtime. Now, the lack of daylight suggested I'd lost more than a few hours since that incident. Apart from the odd situation of sitting here in my car in the middle of the night, that line of trees, becoming clearer in the middle distance, was now firmly rooted where Chris's garage should be.

Resisting the urge to mutter 'amazeballs', I thumbed around the radio button as the BBC newscaster announced today's headlines.

"The headlines tonight, the 30th March. The Prime Minister, John Major, is under increased pressure as calls for his resignation mount following the unpopular compromises regarding European voting rights. Tonight, there's speculation that the IRA are about to announce an Easter cease-fire, which has already been dismissed by Unionist leaders. Germany is demanding tighter restrictions on exports of British beef, disagreeing with other European partners that British beef infected with Mad-Cow disease is

safe. Nelson Mandela has stated that the continued violence in Natal, ahead of South Africa's first fully free elections, would not interrupt the transition of power. Nuclear scientists gathered at Dounreay today to mark the closing of Britain's once most successful nuclear power station. And finally, England has capitulated in the third test in the West Indies, just managing to notch up a total of forty-six runs in their second innings ..."

Open-mouthed, I gawped at the dial. Allowing the information to disseminate through my brain, I attempted to pick through those headlines whilst leaving the newscaster to continue narrating the detail of each story.

Okay, so I'd never claimed to be a huge cricket fan, but a capitulating England team was never far from the headlines. As for mad cows, I was still struggling to work out where Beth and her brother had disappeared to. Regarding the IRA announcing a ceasefire, well, big deal. I'd heard that all before and could recall the news headlines about 'Bloody Friday' in 1972 when the latest ceasefire ended. As for the Prime Minister, now being some bloke called Major. Well, God knows what has happened to that May woman Chris was on about, let alone wondering where Big Jim had got to. And, as for free elections in my adopted country, along with Nelson Mandela being quoted, that was full-on ridiculous. However, none of that could explain how today was March, not August, and specifically my birthday. The big question, though, which year?

That newscaster had opened that bulletin with the words, 'The headlines tonight,' so, at least, that explained why it was dark. Although not where or when. So, assuming I wasn't still lying in that stairwell or in an operating theatre up at Fairfield General, I thought I'd better venture out and investigate.

After tugging up my jacket collar to fend off the chilly night air, whilst totally bemused how the rear-end of the Cortina appeared completely intact after witnessing the flames engulf the boot only a few hours earlier, I strode in the opposite direction from the trees up what seemed to be a boggy lane. I could feel a chill in the air and a ground frost forming, giving rise to suggest that woman on the radio hadn't made an error. Gardeners never had to concern themselves about a frost in August, suggesting tonight was, in fact, March.

"Happy bloody birthday," I muttered. Safe to say, I'd celebrated better ones than this.

While negotiating my way around a seemingly endless line of muddy puddles, trying to stay upright as my trainers squelched through the churned sludge, I carefully negotiated a curve in the lane. Illuminated by the street lamps on the main road, Belton's electrical components factory somewhat unbelievably loomed ahead.

"What the … how the fuck?" I muttered, bemused by the factory's reappearance, before searching through my jacket pockets for my cigarettes. To quote Beth, what a fucktangle.

After patting each pocket and coming up with nothing, similar to earlier when hot-footing through the estate, I tried to recall the last cigarette I'd smoked. "The one Beth snatched from my lips," I muttered, whilst remembering stashing the packet back in my pocket when sitting in that Star-something-or-other café.

"No! I'm not sticking that in my mouth. What the hell d'you take me for, you frigging perv!" bellowed a woman's voice from about fifty yards away, emanating somewhere near the line of trees.

When I swivelled around, I could just make out the woman's silhouette as she held onto the open car door and aggressively wagged a finger at the driver, whose face became illuminated by the courtesy light.

"Lovers' Lane," I mumbled. "Shit, how the hell?"

Earlier, I deduced that Chris's home was positioned roughly where Lovers' Lane would have been in my day. Was I back? Back in 1976, not August, but March? However, I'd celebrated my forty-second birthday with a group of friends on Glen Beach in Cape Town. And somewhere, stashed in an unpacked tea chest in my flat, I had a framed photo of that day as evidence.

"Piss off!" she hollered, slamming the door and dramatically folding her arms.

Not keen on becoming embroiled in a lovers' tiff, I stealthily negotiated the mud track back towards my car, thinking it was time to drive back to my flat and see if this was again 1976. Although I hadn't moved into that dump on the Broxworth until the day Brotherhood of Man sullied popular music, that was only four days from now. I considered being just four days away from normality would be a whole lot easier than forty years.

"I said piss off," she again bellowed as the chap hopped out of the driver's seat whilst attempting to hoist up his trousers. A tricky operation, I suspected, when witnessing him bend forward to presumably safely tuck away his unsatisfied erection before hoisting up the fly.

As I grew closer, their now hissed, somewhat clipped argument held across the roof of their car became audible.

"You said you'd blow me."

"I said I *might* suck it."

"That's as good as a promise."

"I've changed my mind, haven't I?"

"Why? What have I done?"

"It's what you haven't done is the problem."

"What?"

"Washed! You should wash it first."

"Who says?"

"Me!"

"But … your tongue would wash—"

"Oh, God, you're disgusting!"

"But—"

"No! I'm not sucking your filthy dick. Not now, or ever!"

"Fine! Fuck you."

"No chance. You're not sticking that stinking thing anywhere near me."

I winced as I pushed the chrome button on the door handle, hoping to slip silently onto the driver's seat without those two noticing. One thing for sure, the young woman, who I could now see was no more than a teenager, clearly had no intention of saving all her kisses for the chap who'd probably just become her ex-boyfriend.

Fortunately, the girl's verbalisation about her lack of desire to perform oral sex drowned out the sound of my car door opening. However, just like the First World War soldiers' superstition of the third light, the courtesy light gave away my position. Similar to those unlucky soldiers who took a sniper's bullet through their helmets, the illuminated interior of my car gave away my position and halted their heated exchange.

"Fuck!" blurted the unsatisfied youth whilst the girl shot her hand to her mouth.

Clearly not being in a position to slip into my car incognito, I held up my hand. "Sorry. I'm going. I'm not interfering."

"What you doing here?" he fired back, whilst peering into my car and probably concerned why a lone male would be creeping around in Lovers' Lane.

Apart from the lane's reputation, there had always been reports of perverts and flashers trying to get in on the action. Consequently, this disgruntled couple likely assumed I was one of those mac-wearing libertine fornicators, to quote my mother.

"Err …" I paused. To be fair, it was a damn good question. What the hell was I doing here? Placing strange happenings, like time travel, to one side, I bashed on with a slightly ridiculous question. "I don't suppose you could tell me today's date?"

"You for real? You're creeping around like some perv having a wank, and you want to know what fucking day it is?"

"Christ," I muttered. "Look, I'm not a Peeping Tom. I just took a wrong turn, that's all."

Clearly unconvinced with my explanation, he stepped a couple of paces towards me, closely followed by the girl, who now hovered behind him. I surmised, although not of a mind to blow him, she'd figured keeping him between her and me was the safer option.

"A couple of mates reckoned some perv had been lurking about down here, and you in that old crap heap seem just the sort—"

"Why d'you want to know the date," she interrupted her soon-to-be ex.

"Just a question."

"30th March," she replied.

"And the year?"

The chap stepped back a pace and shot his girl a look as she folded her arms across her chest.

"The year," I repeated.

"1994," she whispered.

17

The Calcutta Cup

"Really? Really, are you absolutely sure it's not 1976?" I whined, hearing that balloon deflate in my mind as the momentarily experienced euphoria that I might actually be back in 1976 fizzled away. Although I'd clawed back twenty-two years from earlier, I still had another eighteen to negotiate if I was going to return to my planned morning. Namely, making a tonne of cash by selling some diamonds.

Bollocks.

"I'm off. I ain't hanging around this nutter and, if you're still not going to give me a BJ, you can sodding well walk home."

"You can't leave me here with him!" she blurted, staggering backwards. Although this end of the lane was devoid of any illumination, the whites of the girl's eyes radiated fear which could rival Janet Leigh's terror-stricken face when taking a shower.

"Hey," I trotted forward, reaching out to grab the lad's arm. "You can't leave your girl out here in the dead of night." Unfortunately, the tyre-rutted mud tracks twisted my ankle as I lunged forward. My trainer sank into the mud, sending me off balance and rather unceremoniously onto my arse and into a puddle. "Shit!" I exclaimed, which seemed an apt response going by the smell of whatever unpalatable mess squelched between my fingers as I spun around into a kneeling position.

When contemplating which type of animal's less-than-savoury offering I'd been rolling around in, I helplessly watched as the lad approached his car whilst the girl followed behind. The poor girl tottered along as she carefully picked her way through the quagmire, negotiating the difficult terrain like a tightrope walker dangerously wobbling on a high wire. Although not facing death via a high fall if she failed to hold an upright position, her apparent lack of skill in funambulism would surely result in a mud bath.

"Wait, please," she pitifully whined, halting her stumbling skitter. Presumably, equally concerned about the prospects of a mud bath as being abandoned by her frustrated boyfriend.

"Oi, you moron," I hollered whilst attempting to gain purchase in the mud with my trainers, trying, although failing, to scramble into an upright position. "You can't leave her here."

Unfortunately, my barked command only served to startle the young woman, resulting in a turned-over ankle and an ungainly sideways slide into a puddle. Going by the height achieved by the resulting splash, quite a sizeable one at that. The poor girl received a further double helping of muddy slurry as the tyres on the lad's car sped past.

"Fucking wanker! I'll cut your bollocks off, you total twat, arse-wipe, knob-end fucker!"

Although I needed to wipe the puddle water from my face, I resisted the urge to use my hands, clear in the knowledge that whatever coated them would be significantly worse than what tantalisingly hovered at the end of my nose. Whilst contorting my face to encourage whatever to drop free, I contemplated the young lass's vocabulary suggested she wasn't the sort to take home and introduce to your mother. Also, she'd probably give that Beth woman, twenty-two years in the future, a run for her money.

After gingerly hauling my sodden body to my feet, I carefully extracted my handkerchief from my jeans pocket. After scrubbing my hands and rubbing my nose on the dry portion of the lining of my jacket, I made my way over to the poor drowned rat, who remained in a kneeling position in that pool of slurry.

"Don't–you–come–near–me," she hissed through the tangled mass of hair that hung limply over her eyes.

After Beth's comments earlier today regarding her son's projectile vomiting prowess and reference to that horror movie, the woman now wallowing around in that mud pool with her bedraggled hair covering her face reminded me of Regan MacNeil in that head-turning scene. For sure, if Sarah considered *Jaws* scary, well, I guess my Bay-City-Roller-loving date would most probably faint if she ventured to watch *The Exorcist*.

"Err ... you need a hand?" I offered from a safe distance whilst assessing the swamp-like terrain of the no-man's-land between our two entrenched positions.

"I said piss off, you pervert."

Taking care not to end on my arse again, I carefully stepped back a pace and held my hands up in a placating manner. "Hey, no problem. I was just offering to help, that's all. I'm not a—"

"I said get back! I'm quite capable of standing without your pervert hands all over me," she barked her interruption whilst waving her outstretched arms in an attempt to achieve some balance as she hauled herself upright.

"Alright, alright. Jesus, I was just offering to help. And just for your information, I'm not a damn pervert."

"As you can see, I don't need any help. Thank you very much!" she announced, now fully upright with her arms stretched wide, looking like a scrum-half who'd just been trampled by a couple of opposing props at Twickenham on a wet day in January. "I'm fine! Just bloody fucking peachy!"

Going by the extent of her shivering, I very much doubted her claim. I wrestled out of my jacket and held it out before taking a pace forward. "Here, take this. You look frozen."

"No thanks, I'm fine."

"Are you?"

"Yes! And stay back."

"Okay. It's just you look to be shivering, that's all."

"No!" she fired back, wiping her sleeve across her face. "Oh, fuck it," she hissed, before exaggeratingly gagging, interspersed with blowing a couple of raspberries and finishing off with a round of spitting. "Oh, yuk!"

"Yeah, I don't think it's just mud down there."

"Fucking brilliant. Jesus, fucking dog shit!"

"Look, I'll drive you home if that helps?"

"Woah, no way, you perv," she threw back, before chaotically backing up and scrambling away up the lane. A dozen squelchy steps forward, followed by a half-somersault and a yelp, she was down again, splashing into the next puddle via a well-executed belly flop. The poor girl had morphed from her high-wire act to that of a Stupidus clown.

Throwing caution to the wind and hoping not to join her, I hopped, skipped and jumped around the puddles, just making it in time to pull her shoulders up and stop her from drowning in a couple of inches of slurry.

"Get off!" came the gargled response as she shot her head around, her face now resembling that of one of the *Black and White Minstrels*.

"Come on. I'm not going to do anything to you." I hauled her up and wrapped my jacket around her shoulders.

"My bag," she tearily whimpered when pointing to her handbag, which lay embedded in the mud like an unexploded bomb and offered a sucking sound as I plucked it from its half-buried position.

"Bloody hell, what a mess. Come on, I'll drive you home. I expect your parents will be worried sick."

She offered a slight nod when taking hold of my proffered arm as I proceeded to guide the mud-slick girl towards the Cortina. After opening the passenger door, I grimaced as her slurry-drenched jeans acted as a lubricant when slithering her backside onto the passenger seat. Notwithstanding the impending mess, probably needing to employ the services of a hose and shovel to clean the car's interior, I considered a shit-mud-mixture splattered interior was well down the list of my current concerns. Despite now having a young lady to escort home, the small matter of being in 1994 took precedence over that little issue.

By the time I'd squelched around to the driver's side, she'd lit a cigarette and tipped her head back over the top of the seat.

"Oh, could I have one of those? I've bloody lost mine."

She held her hand out, offering the green and white coloured packet and a box of matches. "Help yourself."

"Cheers," I chuckled, pleased to see that the packet didn't sport a picture of a grave, as had the ones Chris bought me earlier today. Well, not today, more like twenty-two years, four months, and thirteen days in the future. "Oh no," I muttered.

"What?" she apathetically groaned after taking a drag whilst keeping her head in that tipped-back position.

"Consulate! Bloody menthol."

"If you haven't got any, then I don't think you're in a position to be that picky."

"Bloody hell," I muttered before lighting one up. Jesus, if today wasn't already bad enough, now I had to smoke a ruddy menthol cigarette.

"Look, mister," she scraped her mud-streaked hair from her face before swivelling her right eye in my direction. "If you're going to rape and murder me, can you get on with it? If not, and you are just going to be a gallant gent and drive me home, d'you think you could shut up and get on with that."

As she finished her spiel, the interior light faded. I reached up and snapped it back on. Whilst studying her face, I took a couple of Polo-mint-infused drags on my cigarette.

"Oh, shit," she hissed, swivelling her eye at me again. "I take it, by the look on your face, you do plan to kill me," the tremor in her voice clear to hear.

"It can't be," I muttered. Despite her dishevelled appearance, the usual result that tends to happen after rolling around in muddy puddles, the girl looked familiar.

"What? What you gawping at?" she blurted, shooting her head up and searching for the door release. "Christ, I know I don't look my best, but what the hell are you staring at? You are some perv, aren't you?" She shot me a look whilst pulling the lever.

"Hang on. Just remind me of the date."

"Christ. Nutter." Rather than hop out, she appeared to concentrate on my face whilst taking a couple of hearty tugs on her cigarette. "Am I going to die? It's my dad's birthday … I can't die on his birthday."

"No! I'm not going to bloody well kill you."

She stabbed the air between us with her cigarette. "I should have just sucked him off. At least that would have been better than a mouth full of dog shit. Perhaps then I wouldn't have ended up raped and murdered by Fairfield's version of the Yorkshire Ripper."

"Who?"

"You're taking the piss?" Still with her cigarette poised, probably ready to thrust into my eye socket if I made a move on her of the sort she was suggesting, she held her position. Despite a sagging jaw, I detected a widening of her eyes as she continued to focus upon me.

"Err … no. No, I'm not. I have no idea who the Yorkshire Ripper is."

"You're joking, right?"

"No. Who is he?"

"Serial killer from ten or fifteen years ago," she whispered, the whites of her eyes radiating that Janet Leigh look again.

"Oh, well, look, as I repeatedly keep telling you, I'm not going to cause you any harm. Now, you said today is your father's birthday, yes?"

"My God. You look like him."

"Your father?"

"Yeah. Fuckerdedoda, you're his spitting image. You even sound a bit like him."

"Fuckerdedoda?" I questioned.

"Yeah … it's my brother's favourite saying. But … how the hell—"

I very much doubted that her brother had uttered that word. Well, if he had, he'd grown out of it. "This might be a wild stab in the dark. But are you by any chance called Beth?"

"Woah … how the fuck do you know that?" she shakily asked whilst shimmying away from me and squashing up against the door.

"Right," I nodded. "Jesus, this is some fuck-crazy day."

"How come you know me? How come you look like Dad?"

"I'm not sure you'd believe me if I told you," I muttered, whilst vacantly gawping out into the night through the windscreen. It appeared this really was 1994, and this terrified teenage girl was the younger version of the mad cow I'd met earlier.

"I might," Beth whispered after an elongated pause.

"Shit!" I bellowed, making her jump.

"What? Fuck sake. What now?" she nervously questioned, her flailing hands eventually grabbing hold of the seatbelt.

"Today's the 30th of March 1994, yes?" I quizzed, reeling around on her and wagging my finger.

"Err … yeah. We've done this bit," she mumbled, fear radiating from her wide eyes as she held onto the seat belt for comfort.

Earlier today, Beth had stated that Jessica had disappeared on April 6th 1994. In less than a week, the daughter I didn't know would disappear from the face of the earth.

Until this morning, I would have said there could only be one reason for that – foul play – however, after my crazy Doctor Who impression, I had to accept there could be two reasons. Although, if Beth's father, that other Jason bloke, had stipulated that no one could drive this car, I doubted Jess had time travelled. So, if this all added up, and I wasn't hallucinating in some padded cell in the loony bin back in 1976, I had six days to prevent whatever hellish act would take my daughter's life.

"Hey, you gonna drive me home?" she whispered, almost pleading.

Breaking from my thoughts, I turned to her and nodded. "Yep," I muttered, before firing up the engine, turning the wheels away from the quagmire that resembled the battlefields of the Somme, and trundling up to the main road.

Although I struggled to accept what was occurring, not helped by my lack of belief in any kind of faith, I began to accept the reason I'd time travelled. Something, or a higher power, had decided I was the only person who could save Jessica.

"Amazeballs," I muttered to my thoughts as we reached the top of the lane.

"Ha, great word. I like that. Amazeballs," she chuckled. "I'm going to use that."

I shot her a look. "I have no doubt you will."

18

Beyond his Time

The irony wasn't lost on me regarding my annoyance at the 2016 version of Beth for her constant use of such a stupid word. It appears that I was the one to introduce it to her twenty-two years before that day I'd met her in my old bank that served eye-watering expensive peculiarly named coffees and didn't possess any ashtrays, let alone my safety deposit box.

If this was 1994, then closed timeline curves could be the only reason Beth of 2016 hadn't experienced this night twenty-two years prior. What had happened to Chris and Beth after my altercation with a dustcart – hell knows. However, this version of 1994 had to be completely different from their version.

Whilst waiting for a stream of cars to pass before a gap appeared to allow me to pull out of the lane, I mused over what reason my namesake had travelled back from 2019.

This was seriously screwing with my head. Presumably, if Beth and Chris from 2016 hadn't made up their elaborate story, Jason Apsley – that bloke who caused me to disappear in 1976 – time travelled for a reason that this unknown power deemed necessary. Whatever task he was faced with, I could only assume he wasn't regarded as suitable to save Jess. Therefore, back in whenever, 2019, 1976, or a thousand years in the future, for all I knew, a greater force had identified that we two Jasons needed to swap places.

As I turned onto the main road, the required direction indicated by a waving of her hand, I considered the possibility that her father was no longer in existence. Just by landing in 1994, could I have sideswiped him into oblivion? That said, if Beth and Chris of 2016 were to be believed, he was alive and kicking in 2015. I shook my head at the ridiculous conversation rolling around in my head. Maybe a padded cell is where I belonged.

Of course, if this situation I found myself in was actual reality, then history, or future history, was about to change. For starters, that letter I discovered in the glove compartment in 2016 suggested that in 2015 I hadn't re-materialised after disappearing in 1976. That Jason chap had written that 'other' Jason, as he referred to me, still hadn't shown up. However, here I was in 1994 – apparently.

"You gonna tell me then?" Beth broke the silence, hauling me from my musing about time travel.

"What?"

"Well, there's a few things that need explaining. For starters, I hadn't noticed because of what's just happened, but you're driving a car that looks similar to the old heap Dad keeps in a lock-up on the other side of town. Also, you seem to know my name, and you look a hell of a lot like Dad."

"Do I?"

"Yeah! A good twenty years younger, but the resemblance is spooky. You've got those bloody great flappy ears like he has."

I side-eyed her as I negotiated a roundabout that wasn't there last night before passing a whopping great supermarket that most certainly didn't exist twenty-four hours ago.

"No offence."

"None taken," I chuckled. "How much is a packet of fags these days?"

"You're avoiding the question. Take the next left, just after that pizza place."

"Come on, a packet of fags. How much?" I pushed her for an answer, deciding not to question when the Star & Garter Pub became a takeaway pizza place. I guess it didn't matter at what point over the last eighteen years that transition had occurred. Anyway, it was a shit pub, so no loss there. More importantly, the thought which had popped into my head was a far more critical question. However, rather than ask, I thought my next port of call would be the top of the High Street.

"About two quid. Benson and Hedges are about that. You can get the cheap shit for about a quid-fifty, though."

"That's a bit better than thirteen quid, I suppose," I muttered.

"What's thirteen quid?"

"Oh, nothing. Look, Beth, I can't really explain or go into any kind of detail, but I have a bit of a problem."

"Next right."

"Okay."

"What kind of problem?"

"You couldn't sub me a few bob, could you?"

"Do what?"

"I'm a bit strapped for cash. I'm hoping tomorrow to sort that out." Of course, that depended on whether I could convince the bank who I was, assuming it hadn't already morphed into Star-something-or-other, or my namesake hadn't already raided the contents of my safety deposit box. There were too many ifs for my liking, but I had to stay positive.

"Oh, err … I can give you a tenner. You have given me a lift home, I suppose."

Beth rummaged around in her bag before offering me the note, which appeared smaller than I remembered.

"Drop me at the end of this road, near the traffic lights about half a mile up here." Beth pointed ahead. "I live just around the corner. I'm gonna need to sneak in the back way and try to somehow avoid Mum and Dad. Hopefully, they're still around Jess's. Explaining this," she waved her hand, indicating her sodden clothes. "Could be a bit tricky."

"Jess, that's your half-sister?" I quizzed, musing that this road was a ploughed field twelve hours ago.

"Err … yeah. Hey, come on. I guess you're not going to murder me now you've driven me home, but how d'you know who I am? And Jess, for that matter. Who the frig are you?"

I rubbed my chin as I pondered that difficult question. The truth wasn't going to cut it. And more to the point, I didn't know what the truth was. "Look, it's difficult to say. I know Jess, although I haven't seen her for a few years." If this was 1994, then nearly thirty-eight years, to be precise.

"Oh … you an old boyfriend of hers, then? Gotta say, that's a bit weird considering how much you look like Dad."

I snorted a laugh at the thought.

"What's funny?"

"Nothing," I chuckled.

"What were you doing in Lovers' Lane?"

"I took a wrong turn."

"Bollocks—"

"To quote your father?" I interrupted, shooting a smirk at her.

Beth screwed up her mud-splattered face. "Yeah. You know Dad, then?"

I scratched my neck, trying to conjure up a sensible answer. The truth being I'd never met the man, but presumably, we had a fair bit in common with each other – oversized, big flappy ears, for starters. "Sort of," I mumbled.

"What does that mean? Oh, just here. Pull up near that bus stop."

I swung the car towards the kerb and glided to a halt. "You sure this is close enough?"

"Yeah, it'll be fine. As I said, I'll need to sneak in."

"Your parents are at Jess's, you say?"

Beth shot me a nervous look. "My brother will be home," she stammered, presumably those worries that I was planning to harm her resurfacing and hoping this added information about Chris might somehow protect her.

Although I didn't want to frighten the girl, somehow, I needed to glean information from her. "Your parents will be home soon?"

"Yes, definitely. Jess lives only a few minutes away in Lowther Close on the Bowthorpe Estate, so they will be back soon."

"Okay." I'd got the information I needed. The Bowthorpe Estate, as far as I was concerned, was a new development just being built. Presumably, it had morphed into a vast housing estate eighteen years later. However, that was irrelevant because I now knew the road where Jess lived. "Look, thanks for the ten quid. You'd better get going."

Beth nodded and reached for the door handle, relief oozing from her mud-spattered face.

"Oh, before you go, just a few pieces of advice."

With her hand on the door handle, primed and ready to make a dash for it, she'd probably decided that although I hadn't inflicted any harm upon her, there was still time. So, as I read her mind, I bashed on.

"Firstly, I think, at your age, boys asking you to perform lewd acts down Lovers' Lane is unacceptable. If you haven't already decided to, I suggest you ditch the idiot. Wait until you fall in love with the right man. Maybe a lawyer called Phil."

"Who's Phil?"

"You'll find out."

"Secondly, ten-year-old boys can be very sensitive. I know because I was one once upon a time. So, when your son, let's call him Oliver, for the sake of argument, pleads with you not to go to summer camp, don't be too hard on the lad."

"Who the frig are you?"

"Good question," I muttered,

"You're not right in the head."

"You're probably right," I chuckled, before what she'd said during the short drive pinged into my head.

In 2016, a few hours ago, when standing on Chris's drive, he'd mentioned that his father used to keep the Cortina in a lock-up. Although I hadn't listened closely to his ramblings, I'm pretty sure he'd said something about his father moving the car to his garage after finding it splattered with mud, assuming kids had taken it for a joy ride.

"Wow," I muttered, gazing through the windscreen, realising that my jaunt in the quagmire down Lovers' Lane had been the event Chris was referring to. I turned to Beth, who, for some reason, hadn't done a runner. "You said your dad owns a car like this one."

She nodded.

"Keeps it in a lock-up—"

"Bowthorpe Estate, behind the row of shops," she interrupted.

Although I needed a car, one to take a trip to the High Street, and two, to follow Jess on the 6th of April to ensure no harm came to her, I knew I would have to park my car in that garage as my final act before – well, who knew when or where I'd end up.

Earlier this morning, when vaulting down the stairs after leaving my flat, I was a rational man. Despite my love of science fiction novels, I knew fantasy from fiction. Now, one day and three time zones later, all that I previously believed

I'd left at the bottom of that stairwell, the point at which my eyes closed after watching two rats rummage around in that chip paper.

Beth hopped out, holding the car door and leaning down to peer at me. "Who the frigging hell are you?"

"Me? I'm beginning to wonder. Let's just say I'm a guy who's somehow ended up beyond his time."

Beth flung the door closed, stomped off, and disappeared from sight around the corner into the next street. I wondered if this Beth would end up differently from the thirty-nine-year-old Beth I'd met a few hours ago. Would my intervention somehow change her life path? Perhaps she would never meet Phil, never give birth to chundering Oliver, and maybe, just maybe, turn out less annoying.

Anyway, if I could intervene in what will happen to Jess, then perhaps young Beth would enter womanhood with her older half-sister still here.

Whether it was twenty years or thirty-eight years ago, when I stepped away from my responsibilities, the day I walked out on Jess and her mother, I now knew I had to step up to the plate and be the father I never was.

As I pondered my next move, I thought of Jason Apsley, that man who'd pinged me off to the future when he landed back in 1976. Could we co-exist in the new future? Had time in 1994 superseded that time of 2016? Had that world now evaporated? That letter he wrote mentioned that I hadn't surfaced. However, clearly, time had altered because here I was in 1994.

As I rammed the gear stick into first gear, ready to head off and check that Midland Bank still existed, I considered it safer if we never met – paradox and all that. After all the baffling events of the day, I thought I'd better reread that letter. When flipping the gear lever back to neutral to reach for that letter from my jacket pocket, I realised Beth had wandered off with my jacket slung around her shoulders.

"Christ," I muttered, not at the loss of my favoured leather jacket but concerned when realising what had just happened – more to the point – what was about to happen. Jason Apsley, in 2015, had penned himself a letter and popped it into the glove compartment of his Cortina, hoping it would somehow travel back through time to 1994.

Well, it had. I'd unwittingly transported that letter back. A mud-splattered Beth would arrive home wearing a man's jacket around her shoulders with a letter written in 2015 secured in the inside pocket. Any mother worth her salt would want to know where her daughter had got the jacket and who it belonged to as she rifled through the pockets.

If that Jason Apsley bloke was a time traveller, he would know that letter to be genuine. Whether I'd thought it a good idea or not, I suspected that this other Jason Apsley and I were destined to meet.

"Bollocks," I muttered.

~

If you'd like to know whether the two Jasons meet, what happened to Jess, and follow the story of that other Jason after he time travelled from 2019 to 1976, then dive into the four-book series where all will be revealed—

Book 1 – Jason Apsley's Second Chance

Book 2 – Ahead of his Time

Book 3 – Force of Time

Book 4 – Calling Time

Novella – Beyond his Time (you've just read it!)

Can you help?

Thank you for reading this novella. I hope you enjoyed this introduction to the story of the two Jason Apsleys. Could I ask for a small favour? If you enjoyed this novella, can I invite you to leave a review on Amazon? Just a few lines will help other readers discover my work. I'll hugely appreciate it.

For more information and to sign-up for updates about new releases, please drop onto my website. You can also find my Facebook page and follow me on Amazon – or, hey, why not all three.

Adriancousins.co.uk

Facebook.com/Adrian Cousins Author

Author's note

I do hope you weren't offended by some of the vocabulary and outdated language used by Jason because that wasn't my intention. Unfortunately, Jason came from an era that was very different from today. In 1976, Jason didn't know any better, so perhaps we can forgive the man for that. Anyway, as he zips through time, I'm sure he will come to realise the error of his ways.

Thankfully, for the vast majority, education has led us to a more inclusive society. That said, even fifty years after Jason's time, we have many more miles on that journey to tread.

Books by Adrian Cousins

<u>The Jason Apsley Series</u>
Jason Apsley's Second Chance
Ahead of his Time
Force of Time
Calling Time (due for release November 2023)
Beyond his Time (Novella)

<u>Deana – Demon or Diva Series</u>
It's Payback Time
Death Becomes Them
Dead Goode

<u>Standalone Novels</u>
Eye of Time

Acknowledgements:

Thank you to my Beta readers – your input and feedback is invaluable.

Adele Walpole

Brenda Bennett

Tracy Fisher

Patrick Walpole

Andy Wise

And, of course, Sian Phillips, who makes everything come together – I'm so grateful.

Printed in Great Britain
by Amazon